Sugar Doll's Hurricane Blues

KALUA LAUBER

ISBN: 1449998488
ISBN-13: 9781449998486
Library of Congress Control Number: 2010900014

Acknowledgements

I MUST FIRST THANK MY husband Celso Lauber. You have been my best audience. Thank you so much for listening to every chapter and plot change with such support and enthusiasm. I love you and our son Celsinho (Little Celso) very much. You are my best friend.

Thank you Gerardo Cervantes for lending me your expertise in writing and grammar. Your honest feedback helped me to revise things that I would not have caught myself. You are a great mentor and a wonderful friend.

I owe a tremendous debt of gratitude to my lovely mother Essie Lee Brown. You always stood up for me and believed in me and I love you.

My deepest gratitude belongs to Angela Fogel who believed in me when I didn't believe in myself. You have shown me the type of friendship which transcends family. You are for me as your name implies an angel. I thank you for all of your help and support from the bottom of my heart.

Thank you so much to my editor Heidi Arroyave. Your professionalism and attention to detail were spectacular. I enjoyed the process much more with your help.

The person who inspired me the most in my life and is the love of my life is my grandmother Rose Lee Hughes. She died before the terrible events of Hurricane Katrina and for that I thank God that she did not see the destruction of her beloved home. She is gone but never will she be forgotten. I dedicate this book to her.

"The Lord is my light and
salvation; whom shall I fear?
The Lord is the strength
of my life; of whom
shall I be afraid?"

Psalm 27; 1

Chapter One

Revelers hanging over the black wrought iron balconies looked like bats in rafters and those clogging the streets were no better. Karl shoved his way just as much as he was being shoved and pushed back and then ducked reflexively when the champagne cork popped next to him, and the fat lady with the bottle in her hand sloshed some onto his shoe as he tried to wriggle past her. Karl wondered if 1984 would be any better than '83 had been. He sure hoped so. After all, he'd lost his job this year, and then it all seemed to go downhill from there. A jazz band began cueing up and so he craned his neck to see if he knew any of the players. Was Charlie there? He always hung out on this corner at night. But the trio didn't look familiar-must be one of them that come in from Mississippi to make money for the night. New Year's Eve brought just about everyone to New Orleans, and the cheap booze that flowed like dirty water helped to open their wallets. Wide.

Karl approached the darkened alleyway with only a moment's hesitation. He elbowed his way through the crush of people. He had managed to be invisible amongst the partygoers so much so that no one commented on his being there. The exclusive club was just ahead of him. Two large white men approached him. Karl moved closer to the wall smelling the urine. The bolder of the men stepped forward and grabbed Karl by the collar, "Happy New Years nigger!" and then undaunted by Karl's blank expression he stumbled away laughing.

Karl smiled to himself. "It's sure gonna be." He whispered under his breath.

Karl walked up the two short steps to the door. He made five quick taps on the door. He looked into the small square hole. Slowly the little window slide open revealing two bulging green eyes.

"Hey, what you want?" A voice behind the door asked.

"I got a message for Marsalas." Karl said with as much authority as he could muster.

"Marsalas don't take no messages." Said the voice.

"Oh yeah, so I heard, but I believe he'll take this one." Karl responded steeling his voice. "Tell him Karl out here knows who been taking over his territory. Tell him that Karl got more than enough information from the man himself."

"Boy, since it's New Year's Eve I'm going to give you a head start, but if you don't start running now it's going to be your black ass. Now get!" The voice sounded slightly amused, but the eyes were watching Karl seriously.

"Man would I risk my life if I didn't think I had valuable information? Do yourself a favor and get me Marsalas." Karl stood taller looking at the eyes behind the small window directly.

The doorman waved to one of his cronies in the hallway. "Man come see this shit! This nigger outside must be drunk!" He laughed gleefully. His friend walked out to the door and looked out of the small window to get a glimpse of the boy.

"C'mon man, let's kick us some nigger butt tonight. I already gave him a warning." The doorman nudged his friend who stood silently gazing out at the young man who didn't look like he was drunk at all. Tony was the manager of the place and found himself removed from the petty antics of his employee. His startling blue eyes conveyed a seriousness that matched his handsome demeanor and classy style. His dark slicked back hair glimmered in the light that shafted through the tiny window.

"Hey boy! This ain't no gym, go on and take your exercise somewhere else." The doorman let out a guffaw. Tony slapped his shoulder and they both shared a laugh.

"I got a message for Marsalas. It's big boss." Karl leaned forward toward the hole looking directly into the blue eyes that were looking out at him. He was determined not to be deterred by the little "white man jokes" that he heard on a daily basis.

"Boy, Marsalas doesn't take messages." Tony said dryly.

"That's exactly what I just told him." The doorman nudged Tony in recognition.

"Go on now, get! I don't want to have to mess up my tux."

"Tony, you do look nice." The doorman appraised him.

"Well, you tell Marsalas that Karl here tried to warn him about his territory being took over and about the hit Turner got out for him." Karl stood his ground.

Tony and the doorman both regarded each other seriously for the first time. Tony opened the door and the doorman grabbed the lanky Karl as though he were just a rag doll. Karl didn't put up a fight. Tony looked into Karl's face and saw how young he was. His dark skin was as smooth as a baby's bottom. The doorman dragged Karl roughly down the hallway. Karl didn't appear to be afraid under the massive older man's weight. Tony walked alongside them unruffled.

"Son, you are saying some serious shit! Don't you know any better?"

"I sure do know better man, but I'm a business man. I know what I'm saying is for real."

"A business man? Hell, you ain't nothing but a kid. So tell me Captain Courageous what is your message to Marsalas? Tony's eyes flashed bright with anger.

"I want to see the man himself!" Karl straightened up out of the doorman's grip.

"Kid, you don't have any wants." Tony replied snidely.

"Tell Marsalas that I was a runner in his first club a few years ago. Tell him I'm Karl Bouvier."

Tony looked at the doorman who had regained a tight grip on Karl."

"Hold his ass here!" Tony walked down the long hallway and entered a different world. The New Years Eve party was in full swing. People were dancing, laughing, colliding into each other. The theme was definitively black and white tux and evening gowns. Tony crossed the dance floor between couples. He glanced quickly around for any troublemakers but as rowdy as the crowd was, it was rather peaceful. The kid seemed too unruffled to be just pulling a prank. He thought about the serious things the kid were saying and knew that it had a ring of truth to it. "Fucking Turner…" Tony muttered to himself as he waded through the crowd.

A beautiful blond on the staircase tugged at his arm suggestively as he walked by her. He remembered that he was a playboy and it was New Years Eve after all. "Not right now baby." He smiled handsomely at her. He started to ascend the staircase next to the dance floor but thought better of it and walked back down a few steps to the blond, cupped her face and kissed her softly. "Wait for me. Later tonight I'll make it up to you." The woman brightened as Tony turned away from her. He returned to the stairs and made his way toward Marsalas's personal quarters. This time he did not look back as a feeling of dread returned. He approached the room at the top of the stairs. When he opened the door it was a distinctly separate environment from the revelers. The room was sober and dark, only lit by a single overhead shaded lamp.

There were four men sitting around a poker table. He quickly scanned their faces but none of them were Marsalas. Two bodyguards got up when Tony approached a curtained booth. They recognized Tony and sat down on both sides of the booth. The curtain was partially opened and a single stream of smoke flowed out of it. Tony saw the familiar glass of Scotch on the table and the graceful hand holding it. He entered the booth comfortably.

"I beg your pardon Marsalas, but we have a situation downstairs which may require your attention."

Marsalas continued to watch the game silently waiting to be told of the "situation" that would interrupt his evening. He was not a patient man often known for his violent outbursts. He liked Tony because he was as cool as a cucumber and didn't seem bothered by his often erratic behavior. Marsalas didn't sense the fear that Tony had for him but he knew that he was respected. More than that, he was his cousin.

"There's a boy downstairs by the name of Karl Bouvier. He says that he used to be a runner for you. He says that he's got information about a hit that Turner has out on you. He says that Turner is planning on taking your territory." Tony looked at Marsalas uncertainly wondering if acknowledging the kid was a case of bad judgment. Marsalas stirred then and looked directly into Tony's blue eyes.

"Bring him to me."

Tony nodded and immediately turned for the door completely ignoring the men playing poker. They were important businessmen who were always nameless and who never wanted to be acknowledged and Tony respected that line. He never crossed it.

As Tony descended the stairs, the same beautiful blond was there apparently waiting for him. She pouted her sexy lips and tugged at his sleeve. Tony glared at her in business mode, "Much later baby, like tomorrow." The blond flared anger but stepped aside.

Tony walked back through the even rowdier crowd having to make his way back to the front door. The doorman still had Karl in a vice like grip but Karl remained unconcerned. "Let him go." Tony growled.

The doorman released him and the quiet, patient Karl disappeared, "Told you!" he pointed in the doorman's face.

Tony grabbed Karl's arm lightly, "You had better know what you are talking about or that's your ass. Now listen here boy, I'll give you a chance to run right now. It's the last chance you gonna get tonight." Tony stepped aside and pointed to the door. Karl doesn't respond but kept walking toward the entrance of the club. A place that would be forbidden to him on any regular evening, but this evening wasn't regular; it was turning out to be downright interesting. They crossed the dance floor obvious standouts with the lanky black Karl in tow. As they approached the stairs people stepped out of the way to avoid brushing elbows with a black man. They entered the poker room but this time everyone looked up to see the uninvited intruder. The two bodyguards immediately approached and frisked Karl roughly.

Marsalas stood and came out of the booth. The bodyguards released Karl. Marsalas came face to face with Karl, studying him.

"You remember me?"

"Sure kid, I never forget nobody."

"Mr. Marsalas, I mean no disrespect coming to you on this holiday evening. You helped my family in our time of need and I appreciate it. Now I hear that Turner has been biting off a piece of your action in New Orleans east and there's big talk about bumping you off....no disrespect."

"None taken how is your father?" Marsalas asked.

"He's dead bout one year now." Karl bowed his head.

"I'm sorry to hear that kid. Now, who's doing all of this talking?"

"Sonny and Ramon mostly, they are Turner's right hand men. I did a deal with them last week so the man called me back for something else. The fat one talks a lot so I hear everything they say and then last week I was at the shipyard and I heard Turner say things himself. Like planning to get you out of the picture and stuff like that. They said that they would do it at the Fairgrounds where you play the horses on Fridays. They say that they will take you in your box and that you won't even see it coming. They already set somebody on the job so that you would be familiar with him. He's a big white man named Jim."

Marsalas nodded in recognition. He remembered when Jim started working that box about one month ago, he didn't check on him because the owner of the track said that he had screened him himself, maybe he was in on the deal.

"Anything else?"

"Yes sir, they say that you've got a tight lock on the Biloxi gaming as well. They want to get rid of the guy over there that is your front man and run the entire southeastern part of the country.

"Now how did you manage to hear all of that?" Marsalas asked raising an eyebrow.

"I know how to be invisible and ain't nobody paying me no attention." Karl answered.

"I'm paying attention." Marsalas answered.

He was a man of few words but when he spoke the meaning was always crystal clear. Karl swallowed but looked back into the eyes of death.

"Thank you Karl. Tony, give Karl some cash here for his trouble."

"Pardon me sir but how do you know that this ain't a trick?" Tony asked concerned and surprised that Marsalas was taking the word of a young kid with hardly any other questioning.

I know this boy and knew his father. He's all right." Marsalas answered simply with no other explanations.

"Karl you stay away from Turner and that gang. I'm going to give you enough money to move on and get out of any trouble. You've got a talent for numbers, use it."

"C'mon let's go." Tony grabbed Karl by the shoulders.

"5 G's should cover him." Marsalas said directly to Tony.

"I hope that you are right boss." Tony said still worried.

"Go pay this Jim at the Fairgrounds a visit. Let him know that his job has been terminated." Marsalas returned to the booth and picked up his Scotch. "Kid, watch yourself. I don't forget a favor, ever." With that he closed the curtain.

Tony walked Karl down the stairs and took him to the back offices. "Let's set up your future Karl." Karl stood quietly, relief flooding him. He had done the right thing for himself, for his family. He smiled slowly.

"Where did you get all of this money Karl?" Mona cried shaking her head as she watched him count it for the third time.

"I did a job and I earned it." Karl said with a smug smile.

"Did you kill somebody for it? Is this blood money?" Mona shivered. Her tawny colored skin and long black curls inspired desire in Karl instead of aggravation.

"No girl, I ain't killed nobody. Haven't you told me that a man without money ain't a man?" Karl asked.

"A man who steals is a dead man." Mona said her mouth forming into a resolute line.

"Baby, my skin may be as black as tar but my brain is in working order." Karl looked at her nodding his head.

"What does that mean?" Mona yelled and stood angrily.

"It means that I know that them white fellas be checking you out and you don't have to give them what they want to get what you want. I can give it to you myself." Karl threw money across the bed.

"I don't know what you mean." Mona stood shaking.

"Yes you do. Now tell me is that baby you carrying mine?" Karl put down the money.

"Yes Karl, dammit! Why would you ask me that?" She turned away from him then.

"Curious, that's all. It seems you been going to the French Quarters more than necessary. You are going to start showing soon. It's time to stay home." Karl went to her then. "I will marry you because I love you. Whatever you done before is over now."

"It's yours Karl." Mona asserted.

"Time will tell." Karl looked at the money tempted to count it again.

Chapter Two

"I don't have no time to be babysitting no child." Karl said to the pretty little girl in his arms. She cupped his face lovingly. There was a knock at the door. Karl looked around scared. "I told your mama to hurry up!" He hissed angrily. He put the child down on the couch. He walked to the door angrily but as he swung the door open two young black men burst in grabbing him by both arms and dragging him through the open doorway.

"Daddy, daddy!" the little girl screamed.

During the struggle Karl looked over his shoulder to shout, "Run Sugar Doll, run!" The two men began beating and kicking Karl right then and there. Sugar Doll ran to the bedroom and hid in the closet sobbing. The sounds of struggling filled the closet in a loud echo of screams and muted kicking. The little girl put her hands to her ears to hide from the sound of impending death. Finally it stopped.

The two men were whispering, "She's just a little kid man, she don't know us, let's go!" She heard the men just outside the door. The door knob turned slowly and then she heard them stepping away. "Kids can be dangerous." said a low, deep voice.

"C'mon man, she can't be no more than 4 or 5; my baby sister can't remember nothing you tell her. Let's go man, Karl got what he deserved but the girl is innocent."

"Yeah, all right man. I don't want killing a baby girl on my conscience." The door slammed. After several moments Sugar Doll crawled into the room to find her father's bloodied figure lying on the white carpet. She embraced him with her little arms, then as though she were the parent and he was the child. The door opened again and as Sugar Doll looked up in fear her mother let out a scream.

Marsalas attended Karl Bouvier's funeral. He provided limousines for the family. Mona knew that her husband had had shady dealings but the turnout alone made her realize that her husband was in quite deeper than even she had imagined. She stood at the gravesite amazed that so many whites would pay their last respects to skinny Karl. Old men passed the gravesite and in shaking her hand deposited hundreds of dollars there. Little Sugar Doll had her little black purse full of twenty-dollar bills. One would think that this was a wedding and not a funeral. Mona knew that Karl had been up to something when he'd purchased their home in New Orleans' East almost five years ago but he didn't talk and she hadn't bothered to ask. She knew that he ran around with sluts and tramps but he didn't know that she had her own secret lover and that secret had kept her in the marriage.

Marsala's crew thought that Karl had died for saving his life. He had lost and Marsalas had won. Tony stood next to Marsalas. His rich dark hair contrasted with his flashing blue eyes. He was not handsome, he was beautiful. He could not keep his eyes off of Mona. Her caramel colored skin drove him wild. He was the only one who seemed to be happy that Karl was dead. He could now have her whenever he wanted. When he couldn't he would get angry and no woman wanted Tony to get angry.

Mona looked over the gravesite. She instinctively took her daughter's hand. She could feel the heat pulsing through her veins as she felt Tony's gaze on her.

"You could wait until after the funeral to show your lust!" Karl's mother snapped at her. Mona dropped her gaze. She hadn't realized that she was looking at Tony. The heat rose in her cheeks. She could still feel him looking at her, caressing her from a distance.

"The kid should go to her grandmother's or one of your cousins in the country." Tony argued for the hundredth time.

"No, she's fine just where she is, I've got her in a nice Catholic school and I like to know what she is doing." Mona replied bored with the conversation.

"Baby, do you think that the way we carry on is good for her Catholic morals?" Tony grabbed her by the neck and ground into her suggestively.

"No, you are right about that, but I don't want to lose my baby. I've already lost her father." Mona pouted.

"Lost her father? What are you talking about? You were doing me when he was alive. You didn't care for him. If it weren't for that bar I gave to you, you would have nothing!" Tony's yelled.

"Tony, calm down. I just mean that she needs me now. She was very close to her father and seeing him die like that really affected her." Mona reasoned.

"You know what? That kid has got to go! I'm running things now, keeping you out of the hole. Do you think that Marsalas would let a colored woman run such a successful bar if I weren't involved with it?"

"Tony, don't you threaten me. You sure took over quickly. I'm wondering what you had to do with Karl's murder. I'm wondering if things didn't just work out for you just fine!" Mona realized her mistake as soon as she had made it. Tony slapped her hard across the face. He pushed her down and continued slapping her.

"Don't you ever say that to me. Don't you ever say anything about your beloved husband again. Everything I've done has been for you and you'd better remember that. Who do you think the police would believe, me or a bar running whore?" He pushed a struggling Mona down unto the bed and kissed her on the mouth. She bit him but he laughed and pushed himself on her, keeping her in a chokehold while he forced himself on her. She found herself aroused and responded to his willful thrusting. Soon they were both in ecstasy as Mona opened up to her lover turned murderer. She loved him and Sugar Doll would have to go.

"I'm worried about the crowds." Marsalas complained to Tony.

"What's better than hiding in plain sight?" The bar is pulling the kind of money that would provide a perfect cover from the cops." Tony smiled.

"Yeah, but what about the FBI?" Marsalas asked.

"The operation is too small for their interest." Tony shrugged as he drank down his scotch.

"What about Mona?" Marsalas asked.

"She doesn't know anything. I keep her in the dark about things. She's just happy that I let her run the place." Tony smiled.

"Never think that a woman is stupid." Marsalas advised.

"I make sure that I take care of the books myself. I have it under lock and key." Tony assured him.

"Keep it that way." Marsalas still looked skeptical. He walked to the door. Tony followed him relieved that he'd dropped the matter.

Big Ma stood on the top step as the huge white Cadillac pulled into the yard. A fresh summer rain had just started following days of stifling heat. Big Ma looked on with dismay as her oldest child got of the passenger side of the car dressed in a bright gold dress and heels. She opened the backdoor and pulled a crying Sugar Doll out of the backseat.

"Mama, I want to stay with you. Don't leave me Momma, I'll be good." Mona grabbed the seven year old and pulled her alongside her as she approached the white house with green piping. "Tony get her suitcase." Tony got out of the car dressed in a suit. He went to the trunk to get the case. Mona approached the house. "Hey Momma! How you doing?"

"C'mon here honey. Come by grandma. I've got some nice home cooked food for you and a pie in the oven." Big Ma said to Sugar Doll, avoiding Mona. The little girl clung on to her mother. "I want to stay with you!" Mona pushed her away, "Go on now, go with Big Ma, she'll take good care of you." Big Ma took Sugar Doll's hand. C'mon baby, now you don't remember me, but I remember you and you'll be good company for me. Now come on inside with Mom. Sugar Doll looked into the plump kindly face, which stared down at her and saw the pity in them and the tears in her eyes. She released her mother and went with the older woman. "Go on inside and look at the room I've fixed up for you. I'll be there in a minute."

A little pudgy boy stood across the ditch. "Who is that Big Ma?" He shouted.

"That's your cousin, Sugar Doll. Come over here and get her suitcase from this white man and bring it inside. Go and introduce yourself Bertrand. I just baked a nice pie for ya'll." Big Ma turned back to Mona.

Bertrand passed the glamorous woman staring, "Are you a movie star?" Mona smiled at him, but Big Ma answered him, "No son, this is your cousin Mona, my oldest daughter, now go on and get that case real quick or I'll change my mind about giving you a piece of that pie." Bertrand was a rotund boy but he moved quickly after that. He walked by carrying the case in front of him easily.

Big Ma eyed him until he went inside. "Well Mona, you sure beat all. You're throwing away your little girl like she was a puppy to give away. And for what? This white man here? He don't care nothing about you and you too stupid to know it. What's those marks around your neck?"

Mona covered her neck with her collar. "Now Momma, we talked before I came here and you said that it was okay. If you've changed your mind I can take her back."

"The hell you will take that child back, look at you dressed like a whore with your white man. See I never disowned none of my own children and I am not going to start today but I pray for your very soul Mona. If your father was alive he'd shoot you dead rather than see you living like this."

"Mrs. Jones please know that I am taking very good care of your daughter." Tony smiled smoothly.

"Oh really? So much good care that she have to abandon her own child? Probably yours too from the looks of her. Mark my words you reap what you sow boy. White or not you will burn in a living hell." Big Ma turned toward the house angrily.

"Well Momma, I'll just have to burn in hell because I'm going back to New Orleans and I don't know when I'll be coming back." Mona turned on her heel and was forced to jump a puddle of water.

"One day you'll be sorry and you'll need this girl. I pray to God that she can forgive you." Big Ma went into her cool house to sit down. She was so angry that her blood pressure had gone up and she needed to sit. "That girl, that girl." She cried to herself.

Tony and Mona drove off onto the gravel highway and headed back to the city.

"[illegible] tell you [illegible] take that child back. Look at you [illegible] home with [illegible] white man [illegible] never [illegible] children [illegible] going to start today [illegible] If your father was alive he'd [illegible] than [illegible] living like that."

"[illegible] let you know that I am taking very good care of [illegible] daughter [illegible]

"[illegible] So much good care that she have to [illegible] child. Probably [illegible] from the [illegible] of her. [illegible] that you sow [illegible] Whether or not you will burn in a living hell." [illegible] turned toward the house angrily.

"[illegible] have to [illegible] hell because I'm [illegible] New Orleans and I don't know when I'll [illegible] back." Moon turned on her heel and was forced to [illegible]

"One day you'll be sorry [illegible] this girl. I pray to God that she [illegible] Ma went into [illegible] house [illegible]

[illegible]

Chapter Three

"Sugar Doll, now I know that your momma had you in them Catholic schools up in the city but down here we Baptist." Sugar Doll liked the warm Baptist church they attended better than the stuffy and formal Catholic Church.

"Big Ma when the choir rises to sing I feel so good." Church was a celebration. Living with Big Ma was a comforting thing for the lost child nicknamed Sugar Doll. She grew up on fried chicken and Jesus. She took Sugar Doll out of her Catholic girl clothes and put her into long skirts and head coverings for the Baptist church. Sugar Doll surprised everyone when she joined the choir and sang in a powerful, soulful voice. Sugar Doll was a frail girl with long brown ponytails but her voice had the depth of a thirty year old woman.

"Sugar Doll, you've got to always use that voice for Jesus. The Lord gave you that talent and he can take it away. Don't you get no ideas about singing in those sinful bands like on Soul Train." Big Ma told Sugar Doll one day after church. "Aw Big Ma, I'm not ever going to get on Soul Train anyway. I'm only seven now anyway."

"You ain't fooling me, Michael Jackson's about the same age as you and look at him out there twirling around and singing like a man. Mark my words if that boy don't have problems when he grows up." Big Ma went to the refrigerator and took out a bag of coffee. She kept it in the refrigerator to keep it fresh.

"Now I'm going to make us some chicory coffee and some short bread and we gonna talk about that choir trip ya'll going on next week. I wasn't tough enough on your momma. I thought she was too young to hear about men and things like that. Lord have mercy! The book of Proverbs states it plain, 'As the twig is bent, the tree is inclined.' You gonna be different Sugar Doll. You gonna hear the word of the Lord and you are going to be in the church and maybe one day marry yourself a nice man."

Sunday morning's service was jam packed. The reverend gave a talk about vocations. He was so loud that it was difficult to nod off but after two hours Sugar Doll was sleepy. As they were walking home the familiar church van pulled alongside them.

"We are forming up a children's choir and we wondered if you would like to try out?" The pastor said through the window his lovely suit crisp with starch. Sugar Doll looked at Big Ma who wore a blank expression.

"Well, I love to sing Pastor but I do it mostly to myself."

"Bertrand says that you really can sing. I'd like to see that. He's got a good ear. There's a competition coming up in the fall and we'd like to have our kids ready by then. Ya'll think about it." The Pastor drove off. Sugar Doll braced herself for the lecture about the evils of men and their low down ways, which always ended with, "Look at your mama."

"Big Ma, I know everything, I'll be good and I'll go back to the hotel with Sister Rhea when we are done. Going to Atlanta will be fun. Thank you so much for paying my way." Sugar

Doll hoped that her statement would take the edge off of the upcoming lecture.

"Well that's funny you said that." Big Ma's eyes sparkled. "I didn't pay your way." Big Ma opened the coffee bag and poured the grinds in the top of the old silver coffee pot. She carefully poured the water over the grinds and put the pot on the stove. She didn't like those new fangled drip coffee pots so she kept her old pot immaculate. She then got out the old heavy frying pan and added flour with water and butter. She smoothed it out like a pancake. As one side began to burn slightly she flipped it over. Sugar Doll didn't interrupt the process because she knew that talking was over until Big Ma brought the finished product to the table. She went to the refrigerator to get out a stick of butter.

"Did my momma pay my way?" Sugar Doll asked hopefully.

"No child, your momma don't believe in anything to do with the Lord. The Women's Missionary of Mount Zion Baptist church took up a collection for you. They said that the choir ain't nothing without you in it. Ain't that nice? I been a member for over twenty years and don't that sit me proud? Don't it sit me proud?"

"Really?" She asked both excited and proud of herself. Everybody knew that the "mission ladies" never spent any money on anyone but themselves. Their true mission seemed to be to get out of their houses and away from their husbands. Many of them would pray openly during services that their husbands would die and just leave them the insurance money. Most of the men were abusive or drunkards. There were about seven sad faced men who made up the deacon board who prayed continuously for the redemption of their brethren. Miss Rhea had experienced a "miracle" when her husband Albert suddenly stopped drinking and joined the church. Years later he was diagnosed with cirrhosis of the liver.

"Really!" Big Ma stated proudly. "You is got talent girl, but you must use it for the Lord to be truly blessed." Now eat your food."

"Big Ma!" came a youthful bellow from the yard. "Big Ma!" Bertrand let out a hardy yell from the railroad tracks. Big Ma got up and went to the screen door. "What you want boy, hollering like somebody doing you something!"

"Can me and Kevin come in for some chicory coffee?"

"C'mon then. What you waiting for and why you way afar off asking?" Big Ma giggled to herself. "Kevin scared to ask, but he hungry too."

"Well, c'mon, I ain't got much but some shortbread but that will be good enough for ya'll." Kevin came sprinting from behind a rosebush. They both ran toward the house.

"It sho smell good in here Big Ma!" said Bertrand as he bellied up to the table. Kevin shyly stood by the door. Big Ma's usual swagger disappeared. Her voice became soft and almost inaudible.

"Kevin, you come sit at the table too son. There's plenty of food and if you really good I may fry you up a piece of fried chicken too." Kevin moved to the table with his head bowed.

"You better c'mon boy, I'll eat everything from you if you don't hurry up." Bertrand said gleefully.

"Now that is some kind of truth" smiled Big Ma.

Kevin's mother was what the church ladies called a "bar room woman". She sold her body for little more than a drink and was always cussing him out in front of everyone. His father had left when he was a baby. He was painfully thin and just as painfully shy. No one wanted to take him in as they didn't want to suffer his mother Ida's wrath. She didn't care for the boy at all but she expected him to be home when she got there to wash her feet or to clean up after her. Big Ma was the only woman she seemed afraid of and so every now and then Kevin would shyly show up until Big Ma started looking for him. She would get Bertrand to go and get him. The boys became friends. Bertrand was always so loud and friendly and big. They made a perfect team. Big Ma often called them "Laurel and Hardy".

"I thank you Miss Evangline," Kevin said to Big Ma. He said that he didn't feel comfortable calling her Big Ma so he called her what the older men in the neighborhood did.

"You is welcome here anytime boy. Don't you let that rose-bush scratch you trying to hide. As skinny as you are I seen you." Big Ma smiled. She got up from the table and went into the room. We all knew what that meant, we were about to receive a bible reading.

"Lord Have Mercy, why do we have to hear the bible when we is just trying to eat?" Bertrand asked miserably.

"Hush up boy; I like it when she reads to us." Kevin said defensively. "Then you gonna be a preacher. I'm gonna be a piano player in the French Quarter." Bertrand said proudly.

"You can barely play now Bertrand so stop your bragging, that's a sin and I know it." Sugar Doll said.

"Aw shucks girl, I'm only a kid but I can play now, wait till I turn twelve."

"Michael Jackson could play all kinds of instruments and he was only 8. How do you explain that?" Sugar Doll teased.

"He's got a whole year over me and he's all rich and stuff with his dumb cartoon. My afro is bigger than his."

"Is not." Sugar Doll laughed.

"Is too." Bertrand said seriously patting his afro in a circular fashion. "All the girls want some of this big loving." Bertrand giggled.

"You mean fat loving". Kevin joined in the play. Big Ma returned holding her white leather bound bible with a picture of a blond Jesus on the front with the most beautiful blue eyes Sugar Doll ever did see.

"Ya'll look like talking about loving as young as ya'll are. The only love that is real is Jesus' love. The bible says, "Blessed are the children, come unto me", so ya'll are children and I'm here representing Jesus. So ya'll listen to the truth and the truth will set you free." Bertrand put his face in his hands shaking his head back and forth. Kevin sat up straight and Sugar Doll just listened. She knew that they were going to have "church" and there was no escaping.

"Psalm twenty-seven is for you Kevin. I believe that God wrote a scripture for everyone and this one is yours. The rest of ya'll listen."

"The Lord is my light and my salvation, whom shall I fear, The Lord is the strength of my life; and of whom shall I be afraid?" But then Kevin down here in verse 10 it says, "When my mother and my father forsake me then the Lord will take care of me." You are never alone my boy. You either Bertrand and you either Sugar Doll." Sugar Doll looked into Kevin's face and saw a strength there, a glow that she couldn't understand. He had received the good word from Big Ma. She felt happy that he was there in this cool house on this hot summer's day.

"Let's go play on the levee." Bertrand said after Big Ma went to put the bible away.

"I want to wait for the chicken" said Kevin.

"Boy, she ain't cooking that now, not till the sun starts going down no how. I heard Mr. and Mrs. Truman got a new refrigerator. You know what that means." Sugar Doll looked puzzled.

"What does it mean Bertrand?" Kevin answered for him, "We go and ask them for the box it came in and then we tear it up and use it to slide down the side of the levee with, it's a lot of fun, c'mon, let's go."

"I got to wash the dishes first." Sugar Doll hesitated. It was her only chore so she really didn't feel good just leaving it.

"Man, shoot, come on let's help her so we can all go together. You wash Sugar Doll and I'll dry and Kevin man you put the dishes away where I tell you. Cool man?" Bertrand stood up and put on Big Ma's apron. Sugar Doll and Kevin both laughed.

"Man I look good. I'm so handsome, I'm like Muhammad Ali. Ya'll can't tell me nothing." Bertrand strutted over to the sink and performed a James Brown slide that was very agile for his girth. Sugar Doll and Kevin burst into laughter. They cleaned the entire kitchen. Big Ma never emerged from the bedroom. Daddy was in there sick. That was Sugar Doll's grandfather. He was very old. Big Ma would go in to check on him and to pray with him. The children left quietly.

Mrs. Truman was sweeping her steps when the children arrived. "Hey ya'll, how ya'll doing?"

"We is alright." Bertrand was always the spokesman of the group. "Hey, Mrs. Truman, we was wondering if you still have that refrigerator box." Bertrand asked smoothly.

"I sho do, I knew that ya'll would probably want it so I saved it for ya'll."

"That's mighty nice of you ma'am. We sho appreciate it." Bertrand said.

"It's hot out here ya'll want a soft drink before ya'll go out in the sun to play?" Kevin smiled a big toothy grin.

"Yeah ma'am that would be great." Sugar Doll nodded.

"Well precious, you are just as pretty as a picture."

"Thank you ma'am" Sugar Doll bowed her head at the mention of her real name.

"Oooooh Sugar Doll, she called you your real name. I know you is mad."

"No I'm not shut up!"

"I'm going to go and get ya'll them drinks, ya'll wait right here." Mrs. Truman went inside of the house. Bertrand climbed the porch and sat in a big garden chair in the shade.

"This is turning out to be a great day." He smiled satisfactorily to himself.

"It's easy to please you Bertrand." Sugar Doll said.

"Yup." He replied simply.

Mrs. Truman returned with the drinks. They were ice cold coca colas in the five cents returnable green bottles. Her husband owned a store so she probably had cases of them in that nice house. "I'm going to finish my housecleaning but when ya'll finish put the bottles in that empty carton in the corner. The refrigerator box is on side of the house. My husband already broke it down for ya'll so you can just go and play.

"Will you please adopt me Mrs. Truman?" Bertrand asked half serious.

"Thank you son, I wish that I could but your momma and daddy wouldn't like that and I do so love your father's church." Mrs. Truman turned around and continued sweeping her porch while the children drank their cokes slowly, savoring the cold richness and sparkly bubbles of it.

After they finished the last of the drinks the children did as they had been asked and set the bottles neatly in the carton. They went to the side of the house and there were four evenly torn sides of the box. Each child took a side and began the long walk to the levee. It was about two miles away from Mrs. Truman's house but the walk was going to be worth it, Bertrand had promised Sugar Doll. The entire neighborhood was family. Old relatives sat on their porches and waved as the children walked by in a somewhat marching fashion.

"Hey Uncle Pete, we going to ride the levee man." Bertrand yelled to his elderly great uncle as he passed. The man sat there shirtless his gray chest hair glowing in the sun.

"Ya'll be careful of tree stumps and have a clear path in front of you. You can slide down pretty fast and bust your head wide open."

"All right Uncle Pete, we'll be careful."

"Bertrand, why'd you tell him where we was going? Kevin asked.

"He's babysitting me man. If my momma call and I'm not home she's going to fuss at him. He's just an old dude with nowhere else to go. I feel sorry for him. He's nice. That's why, you mind man?" Bertrand asked genuinely irritated at Kevin.

"Naw man, I see." Kevin shrugged.

They approached the levee which seemed like a mountain to them. "I'm scared" said Sugar Doll.

"Don't be scared" said Bertrand. "You can ride down the first time with me. You can hold onto my back and I'm so fat if we tumble you will be alright. It will be just like landing on a pillow cousin."

Sugar Doll laughed, "You ain't that fat."

"The hell I ain't." Bertrand laughed. "I'm going to grow up and be a wrestler and I'm going to turn this fat into muscle." Bertrand flexed his fat arms.

"I thought that you were going to be a piano player?" Kevin asked. "Man you've got to have something to fall back on and I'm always going to be big, so there you go, and I don't have to go to school or nothing to whip somebody's ass." Bertrand started up the levee.

"Ooooooh you said a bad word right after church Bertrand, you going to hell." Sugar Doll said.

Bertrand looked around sheepishly and then up to heaven, "I'm sorry God" and then he looked at Sugar Doll, "I'm sorry I cussed in front of you cousin."

"It's all right." Sugar Doll got on the large piece of refrigerator cardboard turned sled and held onto Bertrand's waist. Kevin pushed them from behind and off they went laughing hysterically. They slid down well past the bottom of the levee. They fell into fits of laughter. Kevin yelled, "C'mon shoot, my turn ya'll." Bertrand and Sugar Doll climbed the mountainous levee once again their legs aching from the long walk and pushed Kevin from behind. He laughed and seemed to go more quickly than they had.

"See Sugar Doll, its safe and it goes faster when you are on it by yourself. I'm going to go by myself this time, watch what I do." Bertrand got on the cardboard and after Sugar Doll gave him a push he went rapidly sideways down the levee at a high rate of speed. He was grinning and laughing. Kevin had made his way back up the hill. Bertrand remained down at the bottom of the levee.

"Hey man, you push Sugar Doll on her board toward me and I'll catch her." Sugar Doll felt scared but she climbed on and closed her eyes. She felt the hand at her back and the quick breeze that whizzed by her and before she knew it she was sliding into Bertrand.

"Next time keep your eyes open girl." Bertrand admonished. "Life ain't worth seeing from behind your eyelids."

The children played there for hours all of them getting as dark as Hershey bars. They had a lot of fun on that day and many more days of that summer.

Chapter Four

Lower Plaquemines Parish where the former slaves remained friendly with the former masters. The small town boasted an unusually close nit community. Even though whites and blacks did not fraternize they helped each other out during hurricane season. Men who worked on boats together understood that sometimes a man just needed a little help to save his livelihood and his family. The whites had their stores and the blacks had theirs. Free enterprise was booming in the community. A simple fisherman could make a living and keep his trailer parked on his own land. Sugar Doll never went to "the city" to visit her mother and after awhile she stopped looking for visits with the woman.

She sang in the choir of Mount Bethel Baptist Church and was happy for the joyous music she shared with her family and friends. There were really no race problems in the community because of the strong family units there. The blacks entertained themselves and had many family parties and barbeques. The whites had their exclusive albeit boring country club. The only enemy of all people on this tiny peninsula town was the hurricane. Sugar Doll hadn't been born when Betsey had come and devastated everything. Camille was also a horrifying hurricane but the community was resilient and returned to defiantly rebuild.

She attended a segregated second grade when the whites finally decided to follow the rest of the nation. It was a sad day for the black children because their mothers, grandmothers, aunts and great aunts had been the cafeteria workers at their school. Instead of fish sticks they were served fried catfish covered in delicious cornmeal. Instead of bland soup they served spicy gumbo and instead of white rice they served jambalaya. All of those ladies retired and then the students were forced to eat what the state provided. Some things were better left alone.

Sugar Doll was so beautiful that all of the boys dreamed of her. Her creamy honey-colored skin and auburn hair belied her heritage. She looked like a mixture of both her mother and father. She was considered a mulatto although both of her parents were black. Mixed raced people were looked down upon in her community but she was shielded from this by the affable but dangerous Bertrand. Bertrand could make you laugh and kick your ass all at the same time and he usually had people apologizing for making him kick their ass. She was not allowed to "court" by her grandmother and she was in church practically every day.

She found her freedom in her singing and as she grew up she realized that she wanted to sing. She did not want to sing gospel music however, she wanted to sing groovy music like Chaka Khan or Patti Labelle. She would sneak off to the music room with Bertrand and they would have jam sessions. He was right; his piano playing had become expert. He was still plump at 15 but handsome and talented and charming.

"Big Ma! Come quick! Kevin's getting in the police car!" One night Bertrand ran through the sweltering heat to find Big Ma sitting at the table drinking a cup of coffee.

"What for?" Big Ma stood up alarmed.

"They said he stole some jewelry from Miss Becky down the street." He exclaimed.

Big Ma stood wearily and went to the screen door. She saw the police cruiser across the road. The officer was talking to one of the neighbors.

"Go get my slippers under the bed." Big Ma said over her shoulders.

Big Ma, Bertrand and Sugar Doll walked across the road to where the cop car sat idling. Kevin was in the back seat crying.

"Good evening your officer. May I ask what the problem is with this here boy?" Big Ma asked.

"The problem is ma'am that he got caught." The officer said.

"Caught doing what?" Big Ma asked.

"Are you his mother?" The officer asked.

"No sir but I take care of him from time to time. His mother died a few months ago." Big Ma lied.

"Well I'm sorry to hear that but the victim, Miss Becky, has decided to press charges on him sure enough. I was just taking statements."

"What's going to happen to him?" Big Ma asked alarmed.

"He'll go to a juvenile detention center and from there if nobody claims him he'll probably be placed in a foster home."

"Could I claim him?" Big Ma asked.

"That would be something you would have to take up with the social workers. "He'll be arraigned tomorrow over in Point A La Hache. You could come and try to get a bid in then. I've got all I need now. I'm taking him now but I wish you luck ma'am."

"Thank you, your officer." Big Ma turned then toward the car and put her hand on the window.

"We gonna try to get you Kevin, you hear? Take heart and do not be afraid." Big Ma said.

Kevin looked out at Big Ma his round eyes full of tears. The car pulled off then.

Big Ma did try to help Kevin but she wasn't certified as a foster parent and Kevin had committed a felony by breaking and entry so they put him in a group home. He ran away several times but they would always catch him. He kept in touch with Bertrand from time to time but he never came to the Parish again during their childhood. Big Ma prayed for Kevin and worried about him like he was her own lost son and in a way he was. After that first summer Kevin would come over to the house less bashfully and he was always a willing audience to Big Ma's sermons. She didn't understand why he had turned bad as he had been so respectful and polite to her. She chalked it up to grief at losing something he never had, his mother's love.

"We are going to have a selection from the beautiful Precious Bouvier. She is a wonderful singer in the Lord and we here at Mount Bethel Baptist are proud of her. Sugar Doll what will you be singing today baby?" Reverend Howard looked up to the choir stand, "Well done," Sugar Doll said as she rose to the microphone. "Praise you Jesus, thank you everlasting Savior, be open to the Holy Spirit congregation. Sugar rose and began soulfully and slowly singing her favorite gospel song, "I had a dream the other night, I dreamed that everything was right, he called me by my name, he said "Servant, well done, well done…"

The congregation stood on its feet raising their hands and thanking the Lord. The presence that was in the church was strong and the people felt it. Sugar Doll was only eighteen years old but she had grown into womanhood at an amazing pace. She walked down the steps and leaned on the organ which Bertrand was playing. He sneaked in a jazz rift that the congregation didn't seem to notice.

After church Sugar Doll and Bertrand and his girlfriend Tonya began to walk the one mile home.

"I knew I should have brought a change of clothes. I hate to sweat out my new suit." Bertrand sighed at the inevitable probability that he would be fully sweaty by the time he got home.

"It's not that far baby," his girlfriend Tonya intoned. She and Bertrand had been an item for the past two years. Everyone bet that they would get married.

"Thanks baby, but that doesn't make me feel any cooler." Bertrand joked. "I can make you feel hotter anytime you want." Tonya rubbed his shoulders.

"Ya'll need to stop just coming from church and talking dirty." Sugar Doll responded.

"I'm sorry you still a virgin girl, it will happen for you girl." Tonya grinned.

"It better hell not! Not on my watch cousin." Bertrand touched her shoulder. He adored his cousin and protected her at all costs.

"Don't worry Bertrand, I don't even have a boyfriend." Sugar Doll sighed.

"If Big Ma wasn't so religious I would swear she put a hex of me or something."

Bertrand laughed at this.

"I'll tell you what the hex is, it's your cousin Bertrand promising to put a can of whip ass on anyone trying to get to you for just one thing." Bertrand wiped the sweat from his brow.

"Why don't you feel that way about me?" Tonya asked.

"Cause you ain't my cousin. But I love you baby and I'm gonna marry you, ain't that enough?" Bertrand kissed her on the cheek.

"That's more than enough baby.

"Sugar Doll, why don't we go into the city and make some money with your voice and my piano? Those jam sessions we've been having are great. Bertrand looked at her seriously.

"Bertrand, you are dreaming. You know that Big Ma is not gonna let me go into New Orleans, no way, no how." Sugar Doll's step quickened. She wanted to go to New Orleans very badly.

"Tell her that you are going to visit your momma." Bertrand suggested.

"Now you know you are tripping. I would be asking for an ass whipping for sure." She scoffed.

"Ooooooh, you said ass, right after church. You is going to hell." Tonya teased her overly religious friend.

"I couldn't do that if I tried. I been baptized twice, once as a Catholic and then as a Baptist. I'm fully covered in that department." Sugar Doll laughed at her joke.

"What religion is your momma?" Tonya asked.

"Now SHE is going to hell." Everyone laughed at Sugar Doll's joke.

"Why can't you go and see her? Tonya asked.

"She don't want to see me. She just wants that white man and he doesn't want me anywhere in the picture, you dig?"

Bertrand could sense the anger behind the statement. He tried to diffuse the oncoming heated argument.

"Hey ya'll why don't we go to Mr. Edward's store and get a snow cone."

The thought of cold flavored ice sped up their walking. They walked down the lane toward the store and the conversation was over for now. Bertrand had other plans for his own career whether Sugar Doll came along or not.

Chapter Five

"C'mon now! Ya'll put your hands together! Who says the blues is dead?" Bertrand was a handsome, imposing young man now. He smiled at the crowded nightclub. The bar was open to the street so that people passing by on Bourbon leaned into the windows to join in the jamming. "Ladies and gentlemen, Remy Gaudeaux!" A handsome young man with flashing blue eyes straddled the stage. He is magnificent in his performance. The club went wild with excitement and dancing. "Boy, you've got charisma!" came a shout from the audience.

"Now that's a big word ya'll, you got to dumb it down for a country boy like me." Remy flashed his beautiful smile again and continued to sing.

Tonya ran along the narrow cobblestone street to grab Sugar Doll from behind. "C'mon girl, Bertrand already started. He's gonna be mad." Tonya pulled Sugar Doll by the elastic band in her skirt. It started to come down.

"Ah, Tonya, can I please keep my clothes on? I'm coming okay." She giggled at her friend's excitement.

"I just can't believe that your grandma let you out of the house. I'm so happy for that!" Tonya jumped up and down in glee.

"Girl, I'm twenty years old now, she can't tell me nothing." Sugar Doll said proudly.

"You just turned twenty so shut up; I've been twenty for six months now." Tonya pouted as the two girls ran arm and arm toward the nightclub in which Bertrand was playing.

They could barely get into the door. It was very crowded and the sidewalk was full of onlookers. "I'm part of the band, please let me through." Sugar Doll lied. She was just here to hear Bertrand play with the popular new singer Remy Gaudeaux. All of the girls down home had a crush on him. Now she would see in person what the fuss was all about. They pushed through the crush of people trying to get to the stage front. Remy was onstage in a clean cut suit with his tie dangling askew in a precarious position. He was imitating an Elvis move but singing blues. He was too young for the mature song but it suited him somehow. There were many alternative types of music but New Orleans was and always would be its own universe. That universe mixes rhythm and blues in a swirling concoction of antiquated and modern. The brew was refreshing and kept people coming to the innovative and fun nightspots on the strip called Bourbon Street.

"Wow! He's sexy!" Sugar Doll whispered in Tonya's ear.

"Yeah, he is for a white boy, you just remember that." Tonya admonished.

"Girl please, it's 2005! People don't care about that kind of stuff any more." Sugar Doll brushed her off.

"Yeah it may as well be 1965 here in New Orleans. Just cause they mix with us and party with us don't mean that they want to date us or introduce us to their mommas. You'd best remember that." Tonya turned around seriously even in the crush of the crowd.

Sensing her seriousness, Sugar Doll acquiesced, "Okay Super Momma. I was just talking out of my head." The girls approached the stage. They waved at Bertrand for several seconds before capturing his attention. He waved for them to come up on the stage. Both of the girls went to the side of the stage and climbed up to directly behind Bertrand.

"Hey now!" Bertrand yelled gleefully into the microphone. "This here is my girl" he pointed at Tonya while he continued playing the piano.

"And this here is my cousin." The crowd cheered. "And they both can sing, they church girls ya'll." Bertrand winked at the crowd. Remy walked over and grabbed Sugar Doll and began dancing with her while singing.

"Can you sing Sugar?" Remy asked handsomely.

As an answer, Sugar Doll turned to Bertrand, "Lover man" in "G". In her best Billie Holiday impersonation Sugar Doll began to sing, "It don't matter what I say, it don't matter what I do, I can't stop loving that man of mine." Her voice rang out smooth and clear into the audience.

"Why you sure can sing!" Remy took a seat on the stool and let Sugar Doll sing the song. He was impressed. Sugar Doll felt so comfortable onstage that she took it over. Bertrand played the soulful song as she sang. Tonya sat behind the piano rocking back and forth. The crowd was mesmerized by the young beauty who sang so soulfully. As she ended the song the quiet crowd erupted in an enormous cheer.

"Sugar Doll ladies and gentleman! Sugar Doll!" Bertrand smiled into the mike proudly. Sugar Doll took a bow and walked off of the stage. Remy caught her tiny wrist.

"Now Sugar you can't leave us all so unsatisfied. Why don't you sing one with me?" The crowd seemed pleased with this suggestion. "Do you know, "All of Me"? Remy asked.

"Of course," Sugar Doll said and launched into singing it. Remy followed in a slow beat. Bertrand picked up the song and smiled at Tonya.

"That was one of the best nights ever at the club!" Bertrand said as he was closing his piano. There were still a few couples sitting close to the windows but the club was closing. "Sugar Doll you was something else." Bertrand picked up his cousin and gave her a big bear hug. "Come and work here, you could make good money."

"Now you know Big Ma would have a fit. I would love to but I'm supposed to be going to LSU this semester. I'm almost finished." Sugar Doll loved the thought of singing.

"Well, when you finish you should come here and sing." Bertrand hugged her. Tonya walked over toward them both.

"Can I have my man please?" She said jokingly to Sugar Doll.

"Why you sho can ma'am." Sugar Doll smiled.

Remy came around the corner. "Hey, what ya'll going to do now?"

"Man it's two in the morning. I'm going to get these girls home." Bertrand said tiredly.

"It's only two a.m. surely ya'll know that the French Quarters never closes. "Boy you sure can sing. You gave me goose pimples." Remy smiled smoothly.

"Those are real pimples blockhead." Bertrand said tapping Remy on the shoulder.

"How'd you get a name like Sugar Doll?"

"Well, they tell me that when I was born my daddy said, 'That's my Sugar Baby Doll right there!' and it stuck. Sometimes I forget my real name."

"What is your real name?" Remy asked.

"I can't tell you." She smiled evasively. She looked over to where Bertrand and Tonya had removed themselves slow dancing to the music that was on the jukebox.

"Why not?" Remy smiled at her.

"You'll laugh." She stepped back from him.

"Well, if you set me up to laugh it's gonna be tough not to but it can't be too bad. Is it Wilamina? Remy stifled a smile. "C'mon, it can't be that bad."

"It's..." Sugar Doll cringed.

"Bertha?" Remy offered.

"No! It's not Bertha!" She laughed.

"If you don't tell me what it is I'm just going to have to start calling you Bertha." Remy joked.

"It's Precious, Precious Bouvier."

"Well, okay I can see why you might be embarrassed..." Remy teased. "It's pretty, like you are though."

Tonya walked up, "C'mon girl, we better go. Big Ma is going to whip your hide."

"Precious, you gonna go like that?" Remy asked

"You told him your real name?" Tonya looked sharply at Sugar Doll.

"What's the big deal?" Remy asked.

"She didn't tell me her real name until last year and we've been friends for years. Even the teachers call her Sugar Doll, that's what." Tonya said sharply.

"Oh, then I feel special." Remy bowed and kissed Sugar Doll's hand.

"I gotta go home now but it was real nice meeting you." Sugar Doll said blushing.

"Can I call you?" Remy asked.

"Why?" Sugar Doll asked.

"Because I like you." Remy answered

"But you are white." Sugar Doll said innocently.

"Sugar , I like you. Can I please call you?" He said this in a very playful way. He was irresistible.

Tonya grabbed Sugar Doll by the arm and pulled her quickly from the club. As they ran down the street Sugar Doll looked over her shoulder as she saw Remy standing in the window looking out at her. She thought that she saw him wink.

"C'mon girl, what you doing flirting with that white boy for? And you told him your born name. I thought that you would never tell anybody but me and your close family." Tonya scolded.

"It don't matter. I'm never going to see him again. He probably flirts with all the girls." Sugar Doll said this but in that moment she had felt very special. His cool blue eyes regarding her with admiration and passion and humor had been the sexiest moment in her life. Later that morning as she prepared for bed she could not stop thinking about him and the brief moment he held her on stage in his arms.

A Cadillac pulled into Big Ma's yard. "Now who could that be this time of morning?" Big Ma asked Sugar Doll as they both walked out onto the porch to see who their visitors were. "Looks like Bertrand got a ride with some white boy." Big Ma said again. Sugar Doll's heart skipped a beat. She held her breath.

She was so excited that she ran to the front of the porch. She caught herself when she looked behind her and saw the expression on Big Ma's face. She realized that she had better calm down or she was sure to be embarrassed by her grandmother.

"Hey now!" Came Bertrand's customary greeting. Big Ma waved at him.

"C'mon in, I just made a pot of chicory coffee." Big Ma smiled at him.

"You don't have to tell me twice, you got any shortbread Big Ma?" Bertrand hustled up the path well ahead of Remy who followed slowly behind looking only at Sugar Doll. She immediately felt self-conscious. She touched her hair absently.

"What you bring that white boy to my house for? You ain't selling drugs is you?" Big Ma whispered loudly to Bertrand.

"No! Big Ma, settle down that there boy is a singer. Famous in the French Quarter, he is." Bertrand gave his easy smile and headed inside for the kitchen which was filled with the sweet smell of coffee and freshly cooked dough.

"Good morning ya'll." Remy drawled. He came up the steps and hugged Big Ma. She was not expecting this and giggled like a schoolgirl. Her eyes glistened as she looked at the handsome young man. Her misgivings were already disappearing.

"Do you know who Perry Como is boy?" Big Ma asked.

"Well, not personally, but he's a hellava singer ma'am." Remy smiled and sang a bar of a song that Sugar Doll didn't recognize. Big Ma seemed very pleased with this.

"C'mon inside and get yourself some coffee and shortbread, the best in the parish." Big Ma went into the kitchen and put on her apron. She was going to make a new batch. Bertrand was already at the table eating everything in sight.

Bertrand wiped his hands off on a wash cloth that was still on the table. He stood formally and announced as though he were in the club, "Big Ma, please let me introduce you to Mr. Remy Gaudeaux. He is the best singer in the French Quarter. He's a better singer than Perry Como, Elvis and the Beatles put together." Big Ma regarded Remy again.

"Ain't nobody a better singer than Perry Como and that's that." Big Ma smiled and poured Remy a cup of coffee. He sat down at the small wooden kitchen table.

"Well although I think that's high praise Bertrand I can honestly say that I'm not better than any of those fellas, I'm different from them and that's all." Remy smiled modestly. "Now Sugar Doll can sing. What a beautiful voice she has." Remy added looking admiringly at Sugar Doll.

"Sugar Doll's singing is for the church, maybe even a gospel quartet." Big Ma warned, cooling off on her first impression of Remy. "Bar room singing is fine for young men and fast women but not my baby. She is destined for the Lord and a good church going man. Remy, you go to church?" Big Ma sat down across from Remy.

Feeling the pressure Remy acquiesced, "Well, no ma'am, I was baptized as a Catholic but I had too much soul for their choir and their rules."

"I can understand leaving the Catholic Church, I'm a Baptist myself, we follow the bible all the way and I mean no disrespect by that." Big Ma added.

"None taken ma'am, my grandmother would differ with you on that. She attends mass every day that she is well and prays the rosary all of the time. She's always quoting scripture and stuff like that." Remy looked pleased with himself.

"Well, the bible says to judge not lest ye be judged so she sounds like a godly woman...eh, what happened to you?" Big Ma rose to go to the stove.

"Well, my parents happened to me. Drugs and alcohol did them both in and my father was no count from the beginning. I don't think I ever stepped inside a church after my baptism. I do pray sometimes though."

"I certainly hate to break up this church revival and godly talk but we came here to talk to Sugar Doll about some things." Bertrand interrupted good naturedly.

"Aw shucks, you ain't got nothing to talk about son. But ya'll go ahead while I clean up the kitchen. I'll be listening though, just so you know." Big Ma winked and went into the kitchen.

"Let's all go out on the porch to get out of Big Ma's way." Bertrand laughed and guided Remy to the door. Sugar Doll followed. "She can't hear nothing no way. Don't you worry a thing about her." Bertrand poked Sugar Doll in the side and pulled up two chairs for her and Remy. He leaned against the rail of the porch.

"Look here Sugar Doll, you sure can sing. We had nothing but questions about you after you left. Why don't you come on over to Beauchamp's to make some money with your big cousin Bertrand?"

"I got a job." Sugar Doll said flatly. Remy winked at her, she looked away.

"At the Dollar Store? I'm talking making real money singing the blues or whatever other style you want to sing." Bertrand knelt on the top step.

"The blues is for old people. I like alternative rock." Sugar Doll looked at Remy.

"That may fly in the studio but for live performance in New Orleans you have to have some sort of background in blues and you have got it baby. Then you can write your own ticket. Do whatever you want to do. I can manage you." Bertrand was excited; he had really thought this out. "You can sing R & B which is just the stepchild of the gospel music you already sing in church…for free."

"Girl you saw that crowd in the French Quarter the other night." Remy said lazily.

"Sugar Doll ain't going nowhere near that filthy French Quarter." Big Ma appeared at the screen door.

"What's wrong with the French Quarter? They got nuns who live there and St. Louis cathedral." Bertrand said laughing. "Maybe the Pope will put Sugar Doll up until she becomes famous."

Big Ma came out from behind the screen door, "Ya'll can laugh if ya'll want, and her momma turned out bad enough."

"Big Ma!" Sugar Doll reacted to the slight.

"Now, don't get hurt but you must realize how bad things turned out for your momma." Big Ma responded.

"Why you always have to talk about my momma?" Sugar Doll jumped up from her seat and ran toward the levee behind the house.

Remy instinctively got up in concern and followed her. Big Ma and Bertrand looked at each other. "Why'd you have to embarrass that girl in front of Remy?" Bertrand asked disgustedly.

"She has to remember who she is and where she comes from so that she never goes there, that's why. I saw how she was looking at that boy and what's more, I saw how he was looking at her." Big Ma sat down heavily on a chair.

"Hold on now! Hold on cher!" Remy called after Sugar Doll who slowed down but didn't turn to face him. Remy reached out and touched her shoulder.

She flinched at his touch. She turned around abruptly and blurted out, "What do you want? Are you looking for a good time? You want to see what it's like to be with a black girl so you can have something to talk about with your redneck buddies?"

Remy was visibly hurt by the comment but the slight was only temporary. His good natured grin returned just as quickly. "No darling, I think you got talent."

"Then what's all the flirting about?" Sugar Doll asked confused.

"I'm a natural born flirt darling. Now you are pretty, I'm not gonna lie but I got a girlfriend. I wouldn't talk about you to my buddies either." Remy smiled easily holding her at arms length and regarding her carefully. He had a sexy way about him.

"Why? Because I'm black?" Sugar Doll continued with her bravado. She was deadly attracted to the man and she was trying to do anything to insult him, to alienate him, to get him away from her.

"No Sugar, it's not because you're black, it's because you are a lady and you're right, my friends are rednecks." Remy laughed at this and rubbed Sugar Doll's arms in a brotherly fashion. He released her as she stood there speechless. He gave her a playful punch on the arm and they both relaxed and laughed.

"You got a girlfriend?" Sugar Doll asked playfully.

"I sure do." Remy responded proudly.

"What's her name? What's she like?" Sugar Doll couldn't help herself from feeling jealous.

"Candy and she sure is sweet." Remy laughed.

"Now I know you lying. You making fun of my name?" Sugar Doll asked.

"Yeah, you right again, I am lying. But you wrong about that name thing, I can see it on a record now. Sugar Doll!" He mimicked a movie director setting a scene.

"You were jealous for a minute though, weren't you?" Remy teased.

He grabbed her affectionately.

"I don't date white men." Sugar Doll said defiantly.

"Well, I ain't white, I'm Creole baby." Remy grabbed her hand.

"No you ain't." She smiled hopefully.

"Sure I am. C'mon now, let's go on and get some chicory coffee before your grandma gets mad!"

Chapter Six

It wasn't long before Sugar Doll was able to convince Big Ma to allow her to sing in the French Quarter. She would be chaperoned by her big cousin Bertrand and her cousin Tonya would stay with her on the nights she had to remain in the city. Big Ma didn't want Sugar Doll traveling in the rain as the roads were slippery and prone to flood. The club was doing wonderfully and Bertrand was generous with his pay. He was planning on setting up a recording for his cousin. He wanted to be the next Barry Gordie.

Sugar Doll was just finishing up a bluesy set with the band. It was late and she was ready to head home. She didn't see Tony sitting at a far away table studying her. He got up and walked toward the beauty. "Hey kid, you got some set of lungs." He said. Slowly recognizing him she froze when she saw that it was her mother's white lover. "What's the matter? Surprised to see me?" Tony reached to give her a hug. Sugar Doll instinctively stepped back. She knew the sick relationship he had with her mother and she wanted no part of it.

"What do you want?" She asked hoping that he would go away.

"You mother wonders why you don't come to her club to sing." Tony responded.

"I don't have a mother." Sugar Doll said bluntly.

"Sure you do kid. She's doing good too, better than this dump." Tony looked around as though he were assessing the place.

"Call it what you want." Sugar Doll shrugged.

"It's a dump, kid." Tony shrugged.

"Haven't you noticed? I'm not a kid anymore."

"Yeah I noticed, but then your momma wouldn't like that." Tony gave a sly grin as he took out a cigarette to smoke. He tapped it against the pack, an old habit, and lit it. With the smoke curling around his head he looked like the devil. He was still drop dead gorgeous.

"Why are you here asking and not my mother? Are you her lap dog?" Sugar Doll said angrily because in that brief moment she had found him attractive. She felt the heat of him in his expensive silk suit with his dark blue eyes. He smiled easily, "Look kid, I'm trying to mend the rift between the two of you. Don't open up something with me."

"Then I'm not interested." Sugar Doll turned away from Tony. Tony walked behind her standing dangerously close and whispered in her ear, "Are you sure about that?" The feel of his whisper coursed involuntarily down her spine awakening something in her that made her feel ashamed. She shrugged and walked away faster to put some distance between them. She didn't want him to know how he was affecting her. When she reached the stage she turned and looked back but he was gone. He knew. "What is it about that man? Did he sell his soul to the devil or what?" She asked herself shaking off the sexual tension she had just experienced.

"Who was that?" Remy's voice woke her out of her revelry. "Looked like ya'll had a lot to talk about down there. Remy said this pointing to the spot as though the outline of Tony and Sugar Doll was still present. She looked over to the spot and felt a chill come over her.

"No we didn't nosey. He's my mother's boyfriend." Sugar Doll now back to herself pulled herself up onto the stage to sit. Remy squatted down and brushed her hair off of her face.

"You kidding!" "He didn't look like he had no other girlfriend but you and if you hadn't noticed, he was white. I thought you all had a problem about that."

"Remy, don't play around. Of course that man isn't my boyfriend; he's old enough to be my father." Sugar Doll laughed. Remy's usually smiling face didn't participate.

"He didn't look old enough to be your father but then you are young and a virgin."

"I never told you that I was a virgin and besides it's none of your business." Sugar Doll blushed as she looked down at the floor.

"You are a virgin aren't you?" Remy got serious as he cupped her face in his hand. Sugar Doll continued to look down at the floor.

"Well I'll be." Remy said gently and he leaned over to kiss Sugar Doll gently on the lips. He lingered there a moment the heat rising between both of them.

"Are you going down home tonight?" He asked her.

Bertrand came out of the shadows like a phantom, "Sugar Doll, get your things, it's time to go." Sugar Doll jumped off of the stage guiltily. Remy rose to stand but Bertrand walked past him. He went to Sugar Doll and said, "I told Big Ma that I would look after you so don't make me break my promise. You hear?" Sugar Doll nodded and headed to the dressing room to collect her things.

Bertrand turned slowly around to face Remy the anger plain on his usually jovial face. "Looka here Remy, you are a good singer and my friend but I'm telling you plain, you mess with that girl and I'm going to kick your ass and fire you. She ain't one of your play things. She is my cousin and a good, clean girl. You hear what I'm saying to you?"

Remy looked apologetic, "I'm sorry Bertie, I just lost my head there for a moment. I saw her talking to that guy and then I realized that, well….I like her."

"What guy?" Bertrand asked puzzled.

"Real smooth looking character, well dressed, good looking, probably rich." Remy remarked. "Sugar Doll said that he is her mother's boyfriend which is hard to believe but what can I do?"

"Tony M." Bertrand muttered.

"Tony M. who works for Marsalas?" Remy asked surprised.

"One in the same." Bertrand sighed; his attention had been taken away from Remy. He didn't need Mafioso hanging around his club drawing undo attention to him.

"Bertrand, I am sorry." Remy said.

"No worries man, just keep it in your pants." Bertrand gave his trademark smile and ambled off toward Sugar Doll.

Later that night on the drive home Bertrand asked, "What did Tony M. want?" Sugar Doll was pensive thinking about her kiss with Remy and her confused sexual feelings for Tony M.

"He says that my mother wants me to sing in her club." Sugar Doll answered.

"Then why the hell doesn't she ask you herself?" Bertrand asked the obvious question.

"That's what I said." Sugar Doll answered. "I said no anyway."

"What's going on between you and Remy?" Bertrand asked.

"We are just friends." Sugar Doll answered while looking out the window and the lazy warm rain that hit the windshield.

"Didn't look like no friends to me. I saw him kiss you." Bertrand was looking directly at Sugar Doll.

"I don't know why he kissed me. I didn't ask him to do it." Sugar Doll sighed as she thought of the soft touch of his lips. She unconsciously touched her lips with her finger. Bertrand was watching her.

"He is my employee, Sugar Doll, and my friend. Don't mess that up for me." Bertrand advised as they neared Big Ma's house.

"I won't Bertrand, I promise." As she opened the door the yard was soaked with water.

Bertrand said, "Wait right there cousin I'll come get you, let me take off my good shoes. He kicked off his shoes and socks and heaved his heavy body out of the car. He walked through the knee height water and scooped up Sugar Doll in his arms. She hugged him as he carried her. She felt guilty about making him upset. Big Ma stood waiting on the porch; all of the lights were on in the house. Sugar Doll thought that she did this to prevent herself from falling asleep before she came home.

"Ya'll come on inside out of the rain before you get pneumonia." Big Ma said invitingly.

"Not tonight Big Ma, I have to go back to the city tonight. I'll be all right." Bertrand had stepped off of the steps before she had a chance to protest. "See you Saturday Sugar Doll." She waved but doubted he'd seen it as he backed out of the narrow ditch trying to avoid the deep trenches on either side of the lane. They were there to catch the run off water but they too were often full after a simple summer's rain.

That night after Big Ma went to bed Sugar Doll sat up thinking about Remy and the gentle kiss. Her mind kept interrupting with the strong sexuality she had felt emanate from Tony's muscular body as he stood behind her. She tried to shrug it off and felt that it was a sick impulse. "What is wrong with me?" She said aloud to herself. She knew that at twenty-one she was too old to still be a virgin. If she went with Remy it would hurt his friendship with Bertrand and Tony M. was out of the question and shouldn't even be in her thoughts.

That night she fell into sleep uneasily. She dreamed that she was in a white room. The sun gleamed through the windows. The air was soft and warm. The ceiling fan turned overhead. Remy sat down on the bed and began to caress her softly, her body responded to his touch. He leaned over to kiss her. His hair brushed softly against her face as they began to kiss, he gently lowered the sleeves of her nightgown softly kissing her shoulders. The feeling was exquisite. He nuzzled her breast gently teasing them with his tongue. As he mounted her and parted her legs something changed. His body was heavier more demanding. He kissed her with more urgency, she felt as though she would explode from the inside, his lips trailed down to her neck taking his time sensuously kissing and just when she thought she could take it no more he lifted himself and entered her. She opened her eyes to look at him and Tony looked back his smoldering blue eyes boring into hers. Sugar Doll woke up her body still tingling from the dream. Her heart was still racing. She felt ashamed of herself and her dream.

Chapter Seven

Beauchamp's became the most happening place in the French Quarters; it was second only to Mona's. People of all races came into the club. When that sort of success happens it is only a matter of time before dirty hands want to shake the clean ones. Bertrand had long been expecting it so was surprised that he had gotten away with nearly four years of success before anyone came poking around. The first visit was from a well dressed man calling himself Moe. Moe came in early one morning when the only people up were the tourists who couldn't wait till the evening to come down into the quarter. St. Peter's street was filled with travelers from colder climes. You could tell who they were by the way they dressed. They wore Bermuda shorts and ugly plaid shirts or wife beaters and sun hats. It was Christmastime in New Orleans but it was 75 degrees. Most of the locals still wore clothes better suited for the fall, just in case it got cold as the city was prone to do being so close to the river the temperatures could drop fast.

Moe sat down at the bar and ordered a Bloody Mary. The bartender obliged and smiled at the generous tip the man gave him. It was a good take on a Wednesday morning. Bertrand came in to work on his books and he noticed the man when he walked in but he didn't take any special interest in it until he walked to his back office and saw a man standing there. "Can I help you sir?" Bertrand asked. The man did not answer but he pointed in the direction of the bar. Bertrand picked up his meaning and steeled himself for the shakedown he was about to experience.

Moe stepped down from his barstool and motioned for Bertrand to sit down. Bertrand did as he was asked. He sat down quickly ready to hear what he would have to do or what he would need to get out of in order to keep his business. He had been expecting this for a very long time. "How can I help you?" Bertrand asked deciding to keep things light.

"The question is, how can I help you?" The man asked in return.

"I'm Moe Turtsodky, and I've been sent here to talk about your insurance plans."Bertrand felt relieved, he quickly got up to leave saying over his shoulder, "Look man, we've got insurance, fire, flood, hurricane, building collapse, life...you name it, we got it. But thanks for stopping by."

Moe Turtsodky stood then, "Do you have the type of insurance that Marsalas can provide?" Bertrand was instantly deflated. He knew then he was going to have a problem. A real problem because he owed Marsalas money.

"Let's go to my office and talk." Bertrand gave in and the tall Moe followed him to his back office.

"Let me spell it out for you Bertrand. Mr. Marsalas will cover all of your debts down in Biloxi for a share in Beauchamp's. He would hate to see you run such a successful business into the ground. That is unless of course you have his money which is compounding interest daily." Bertrand, a true gambler, did not even want to know the amount that Marsalas placed on his debt. He had been paying through a liaison but he couldn't keep up with the interest. He had no one to tell because everyone was so proud of him.

"How much of a share?" Bertrand asked voice trembling.

"Well you can still be the face of the club but we will run it and a few of our other business interests through the club." Moe whatever the fuck his name was just too calm and as jovial as Bertrand was he wanted to choke him to death.

"Don't give me an answer now; you have twenty-four hours to come up with the money, a substantial down-payment or the deed of sale. It ain't rocket science." Moe got up and brushed off his pants as though he had sat in something dirty.

"Goddam!" Bertrand thought. "This shit is like a bad movie. I can't believe that I'm in This kind of trouble." Never one to be religious Bertrand raised his head with his eyes closed, "Lord, if you can hear me, please send me some help. I don't want to lose my place because of my stupidity. Help me Lord or send someone to help me. It's time I was dealt a good hand." He removed a handkerchief and wiped his brow. His help was on the way but it would prove more than he bargained for in the first place.

Kevin sat squat in the bushes. The grass made him itch. There was one particularly long blade of grass that kept sticking him on his nose. He wanted to pull it from the ground from the root but then that would make too much noise. He had to be very quiet. He didn't want to get caught. He wanted to do the catching. As soon as he thought about the man he came ambling around the corner, whistling the stupid bastard. Kevin wished that he hadn't decided to squat the way that he had. He wished that he could turn around and sit on his butt flat instead of this thinking man pose. He heard the creak and metallic sound of the screen door, its hinges squeaking as the man opened the door. "I've got you now idiot," Kevin thought as he slowly eased his way out of the grass to proceed to the house slowly glancing around to make sure that no one saw him move from there.

The neighbors were just too damned friendly. He could hardly catch the man with these nosey women who seemed to always be outside putting clothes on the line. Zachary, Louisiana was just country. The people were slow and friendly and lazy. It was hard to believe that just a few miles down the road one could go to metropolitan Baton Rouge the big college city. He had to admit that even Baton Rouge paled in comparison to New Orleans for sheer outright fun and things to do. Kevin smiled to himself. As he neared the window screen he saw his mark sitting on a couch. The woman he was with was perched on his thighs doing some shimmy shake dance. Kevin watched for a minute just to enjoy the scenery. The girl wasn't half bad looking and she'd agreed on a small price to participate in this scam. He readied his camera for the money shot.

She was removing his shirt and actually turned toward the window and looked dead into Kevin's eyes. "Was she flirting with him? Later baby, later." He ducked out for a minute because he was afraid of being seen. Sweat trickled down the middle of his back; he realized that he was nervous. This was big. He gave a nervous glance around to see if anyone saw him. It was 10 o'clock in the morning so most ladies had finished their housework and were napping or watching their "stories" or soap operas. The mayor of Baton Rouge took off his shirt as the floozy bent down to suckle his nipple. That was it. He was unmistakable. He got a clear shot but took at least five for safety. This was going to be easy money.

He stood upright and smiled into the window. "Thank you Mayor Thompson, you the man." The mayor bolted up pushing the girl to the floor. Kevin took off running laughing as he went. The mayor ran out of the house forgetting himself as he ran his pants falling awkwardly around his fat thighs. Kevin turned around running backwards shooting pictures as he went. The nosey women of the neighborhood came out on their porches to see what the commotion was all about thus giving Kevin cover. The mayor came to his senses and ran inside pulling up his pants. Kevin laughed all the way home. It was the most fun he had had in years.

The pictures were beautiful. Professional even, Kevin knew the drill, threaten to tell the wife but in this case he decided to threaten to tell the public. If there was one thing that he knew it was that white women would never leave a man of power. She probably knew what was going on in the first place and was relieved that she didn't have to do the work herself. He was fat and unattractive so she was with him for the money. They didn't even have kids. Kevin felt no guilt putting the squeeze on the mayor. When he called his offices the mayor answered himself, breathless, eager to please. "Do you know who this is?" Kevin asked slowly drawling his words in a Texan accent.

"Yes sir, I think that I do know. How can I be of service to you?" The mayor asked. Kevin could feel the sweat come down the mayor's face. He rather enjoyed this feeling of power over someone else.

"Well, you could give me a couple of thousand dollars to keep your little tryst with the lady hushed up. We wouldn't want anything to interfere with your re-election, especially not your dick." Kevin laughed at his little joke.

"Son, you need to understand that I have very powerful friends and I could actually cause you a lot of damage." The mayor spoke powerfully as he sat alone in his office.

"Damage? The only damage that is going to be experienced is the damage to your career if you don't pay up, now. I was going to give you a week but now that you have threatened me I will give you until 5 p.m. today. If I don't receive $50,000.00 by the day's end these beautiful pictures are going into the Times Picayune." Kevin was tempted to hang up but he wanted to hear the mayor back pedal.

"I saw you boy. I know who you are Kevin Johnson. As I said before if you keep bothering me I'm going to send my "friends" after you. You've got a rap sheet a mile long and so does your mother. You don't want me to go investigating her now do you? Drugs in Louisiana, ain't that a shame?" The mayor smiled into the phone.

Kevin felt the shock of this turn around course through his body. He recovered "I'm going to sell them to the Times Picayune."

"For a hellava lot less I wager." The mayor continued confident that he had won.

"Maybe so, but the truth is that I don't like you and I will probably just give them for free." Kevin said.

"You just do that but then where are you going to hide from me? It took only fifteen minutes for me to identify your photo at the police station where by the way I said that you mugged me and took my wallet. Do you know that it's dangerous to mug the mayor?"

"All right, so you got me but I'm turning in the photographs to the newspaper anyway." Kevin said defiantly.

"Go ahead then, I call you on your bluff. I don't care what the hell you do. It will only make me more popular. The people of Baton Rouge do so love a good scandal." The mayor played his trump card and hung up confident that he would not suffer the consequences.

Kevin stood in the phone booth stunned. He looked at his beat up old Ford sitting there. A police car drove slowly by looking at him. He got out of the phone booth and tipped his hat to the officer who returned the gesture and drove off. Kevin got into his car, nervous, disappointed and aggravated with himself. He drove off. He had not anticipated that the mayor was a rascal. He felt foolish and broke. He knew that in this small town he would stick out like a sore thumb. He had only one place he could go for safety's sake, Beauchamp's.

"He's leaving, yes, should I pursue him?" Officer Dan called the office.

"Follow him until he gets into Baton Rouge. When he gets on Florida Boulevard, detain him there. Take whatever he has in the car and rough him up a bit, or a lot I don't care." The mayor hung up the phone without saying goodbye.

"Sure thing bro." Officer Dan drove slowly down the highway. He was sure that his brother-in-law had not been completely honest with him. What was all of the hush, hush about anyway? If he had been mugged why not make a full report? He didn't know what was going on but he was going to find out.

Kevin drove steadily as he turned onto Florida Boulevard, fingering the photographs. "All of those poker terms, he must be bluffing." He said to himself. He probably didn't even call the police. But Kevin wasn't interested in turning the mayor in and creating a scandal. He truly just wanted the money. A flash of blue lights interrupted his thoughts. "Damned!" Kevin pulled over on the shoulder.

A tall, young officer walked toward his car. He leaned into the window. "License and registration please." He said as he scanned the interior of Kevin's car.

"What's the problem officer?" Kevin asked calmly never looking the officer in the eye but recognizing him as the same officer who he had nodded to earlier.

"The problem is that we don't like muggers in our part of the woods. Particularly not blackmailing ones." Dan backed up from the door. "Tell me just how did you think that you were going to get away with this?"

Kevin shrugged and handed over the pictures. "Could you please just let me go and forget all of this?"

"I could do a lot of things but right now I'm arresting your black ass. Step out of the car please." The officer stepped aside to allow Kevin to get out of the car.

Kevin didn't need to be told to raise his hands over his head. He knew the drill.

Chapter Eight

Remy saw Bertrand sitting at the bar looking dejected. "Hey man, what's bothering you? Why don't you just let it all out?" Bertrand grunted and pushed a bar stool in Remy's direction.

"Man I wish I could tell you, it would make things easier for me." Bertrand sighed heavily and took a deep drink of whiskey.

"Then I'm your man, tell a brother." Remy smiled but his eyes were steady and serious.

"I'll tell you this much, man you are a great singer. I see great things in you and I think that you are better than this place. I want to cut an album with you as soon as my studio is up and running." Bertrand smiled easily his troubles momentarily lifted.

"Are you trying to fire me boss?" Remy smiled and patted Bertrand on the shoulder.

"No bro, but I am having what you might call Fi Nan Cial difficulties. I meant what I said about your singing on an album. Your shit is tight." Bertrand looked over Remy's shoulder to the door at passing tourists. The quarter was never really ever quiet he mused.

"What are you talking about? The bar is packed every night. You aren't gambling again are you?" Remy looked at his buddy concerned.

"No man, c'mon now, why you getting all serious? Let me get you a beer." Bertrand lifted heavily from the stool and went behind the empty bar to the freezer. He took out an ice cold beer and handed it to Remy who took it warily.

"Bertrand man, I thought that you'd given that shit up." Remy shook his head as he took a long draw of his beer.

"I know huh?" Was all Bertrand could manage.

"How much you owe this time?" Remy turned his seat away from the bar and faced the open windows of the French Quarter.

"Too much man. I don't know what I'm going to do. I'm into Marsalas for big money."

"Damn man. Damn." Remy put the beer down on the bar and stood up.

"I could lose the place Remy." Bertrand said. "Don't tell Sugar Doll."

"I won't man but you've got a good thing here and to throw it all away on the roll of the dice is just well..." Remy looked disgusted.

"Stupid I know."

One of the tourists walked into the empty bar, it was mid-morning so there was usually no traffic in the bar until noon. Bertrand usually manned the bar for those looking for the "hair of the dog" remedy. "Hey brother!" Bertrand shouted in his friendly, welcoming voice. What's your poison?"

"Man who you hollering at 'Fat Boy'!" The man said laughing.

"Now that's uncalled for." Remy said walking toward the stranger.

"Kevin?" Bertrand burst from around the bar as fast as his fat body would take him. "Man, you ole criminal! When did you get out? I'll be God Damned!" Bertrand pushed Remy aside and literally picked Kevin up into the air.

"Oh I see, a family reunion. Well I'll leave ya'll to it." Remy said as he headed out of the door.

"Wait man, let me introduce you to my boyhood friend! He is just like family Bertrand said hugging Kevin sideways. Remy this is Kevin, Kevin Remy." Bertrand smiled happily.

"You hang out with white boys now?" Kevin smiled easily. "No offense." Kevin nodded to Remy.

"None taken. Well ya'll, it's been fun but I got to run. Nice to meet you Kevin." The two men shook hands and Remy walked out into the sunny morning.

"Man where you been hiding?" Bertrand looked earnestly at his friend.

"I been busy man. I was up in Baton Rouge for awhile and I ran into a little trouble. I got out of it though." Kevin smiled.

"Ole weasel man, tell me what happened and I'll get us a beer, it's time to celebrate." Bertrand went behind the bar, a new spring in his step. He opened the beers quickly ready to hear one of Kevin's adventures. "You never let a niggah down man, anything I do you can top it."

"Bertrand man I had a sweet idea about that ole rascal Mayor Thompson. You know he loves mixing the honies but no one has ever caught his ass in the act. I staked him out for awhile and I discovered he had the gal in Zachary." Kevin grinned thinking about it.

"Kev man, weren't you afraid of the Secret Service?" Bertrand asked.

"Man, they only work for the president and trust me this man didn't want nobody to know where he was going. He was as they say, 'Out of Order!" Kevin giggled.

"So you followed him and then what?" Bertrand asked.

"Well then my friend I met his lady love Sha Keisha. A young girl about 16 or 17. She's wise though, let me tell you. It was easy. I approached her and came up with an idea of black-mailing him. Hell hath no fury. He was still dipping in the wrong pool and she'd heard that he was about to go to different pastures. So she told me when he was coming to see her again. I showed up camera in hand and got some sweet pics. Trouble began when he saw me!" Kevin laughed.

"He saw you man, was he naked?" Bertrand laughed incredulously the alcohol catching up with him.

"Buck naked and let me tell you that is one yellow niggah! His ass is as wide as some of our home girls!" Both men burst into uncontrollable laughter. "Wait it gets better, the niggah came after me man!"

"Naked?" Bertrand asked in glee.

"Naked and trying to pull his pants on. He ran right up the street." Kevin said chuckling remembering it.

"What did you do?" Bertrand's eyes were wide as saucers.

"Niggah what do you think I did, I ran, laughing my ass off. He almost caught me." The two men stared at each other for a minute and then burst into another fit of uncontrollable laughter. Kevin had tears rolling down his cheeks as he continued the story.

"Man, I got to the car and looked back and there was the mayor of Baton Rouge struggling with his pants and running back to the house. That was the most fun I've had since we were kids man."

"So you have the photos man? What you gonna do, blackmail his ass?" Bertrand asked seriously.

"Naw man, I'm not finished with the story." Kevin thought back to the previous week with delight.

"What else could happen?" Bertrand asked confused.

"So there I was driving down Florida Boulevard about to get on the I-10 when this cop comes up behind me with lights flashing."

"Man you ain't never had no luck, you always get caught." Bertrand looked resigned, the humor draining out of him.

"Will you let me finish the story?" Kevin threw his arms up in the air.

"Go ahead, I already know the ending." Bertrand sighed.

"No you don't niggah. So anyway, the police officer comes up to the window and asked me where I was going. I told him New Orleans. He asked for my license and registration, the usual. Then he tells me that they don't like no blackmailing niggahs up there."

Bertrand looked stunned, "He knew?"

"And then some, he took the photos and put me in the backseat of the cop car. So I'm thinking, 'Damn back to jail I go'. Then he got on the radio to say that the wrong man had been caught. He sat in the front seat of that cop car and looked at the photos and then he handed that shit back to me." Kevin said.

"Now I know you lying. Why did he do that?" Bertrand looked interested.

"He said, 'That son of a bitch is married to my sister. She doesn't deserve this. I tell you what I'll let you go if you promise to give those to the newspaper. She wouldn't believe me if I told her but she'll believe that shit. I feel really bad for her since our momma died. This way she can take him to the cleaner's. Then he opened the back door and let me out of the car."

"That's all? What else?" Bertrand asked.

"He told me that if I just use it to blackmail the mayor he would find me and kill me clean." Kevin nodded.

"Why didn't he just take the photos himself?" Bertrand asked.

"I suppose he didn't want his sister to find out that he had anything to do with it." Kevin answered.

"What did you do with those photos?" Bertrand was riveted by this story.

"I sent copies to the Times Picayune, the Baton Rouge newspapers and to his house." Kevin took a drink of his beer.

"To his house niggah?" Bertrand asked in shock.

"I figured that his wife had the right to know before the news struck. I know how that officer feels. I think that if it weren't for the bad men in my mom's life that she would have been a halfway decent woman instead of a drug addict." Kevin sighed.

"So you didn't get any money from the deal?" Bertrand asked.

"No, but I got the best story ever and the best laugh I've had in years. I'll make money some other way." Kevin replied and the two men toasted their beer bottles and chuckled.

Sugar Doll hadn't seen her mother since she was a teenager. She used to pray that her mother would come to see her when she was in high school. She would look into the audience for the familiar face when she sang in musicals but never once did her mother make an appearance. Now the shoe was on the other foot. She was within walking distance from her mother's bar but she vowed she would never go there. Tony's visit echoed in her head for weeks. She tried to make sense of it but could not.

"Hey pretty, when are you going to dinner with me?" Remy asked as he placed his hands on her shoulders.

"When you ask me." Sugar Doll answered.

"Well I'm asking." Remy smiled handsomely.

"Asking what?" Sugar Doll teased.

"Would you Precious Bouvier, accompany me to Le Beaudreu for dinner?""Well since you put it like that, no." Sugar Doll laughed.

"No, why not?" Remy asked.

"I need advanced notice, like perhaps a week."

"Is Friday night enough time?" Remy looked hopeful.

"I'm performing Friday." Sugar Doll toyed with his jacket.

"What about Saturday?" Remy asked.

"You perform Saturday." Sugar Doll smiled.

"Monday?" Remy asked.

"Monday might work." Sugar smiled and went back to the dressing room.

"Man she is driving me crazy!"

The show was a success and the place was packed again. Bertrand was noticeably absent. He was always in the bar. No one knew where he was and this had Remy worried. He helped the night manager to close the bar at 4 a.m.

"This is just not like Bertrand. He didn't call or anything." Royal said as he locked up the money for the evening.

"He usually takes Sugar Doll home." Remy commented. He walked out to the front to see Sugar Doll sitting by the stage.

"Hey girl, do you need a ride?" Remy offered.

"No thanks, Bertrand always brings me home, it's kind of far from here." Sugar Doll smiled.

"I know where you live country girl. I don't mind, I'm not working tomorrow or I should say today." Remy walked over to her and took her hand. "C'mon let me give you a ride, you look tired."

"Thanks, thanks a lot." Sugar Doll smiled.

They drove mostly in silence for the first twenty minutes. Remy broke the silence. "Where do you think Bertrand is right now?" He asked.

"Well, Kevin is in town so maybe they are together somewhere. You never know, when we were kids they were as thick as thieves." Sugar Doll smiled.

"Thieves being the operative word. This Kevin has a record or something?" Remy frowned.

"Oh he would never do anything to Bertrand. He's like family." Sugar Doll smiled again.

"Like family, I've heard that before." Remy looked reluctant.

"Well in this case it is true." Sugar Doll said.

"There is a wharf right down that lane, Bertrand took me there, have you ever been there?" Remy asked.

"No, I never liked fishing." Sugar Doll answered.

"How about we watch the sun rise together? It's about that time. What do you think?" Remy had already started to turn the car in that direction.

"Okay, I guess." Sugar Doll felt her heart speed up a little.

The lane was long and the shells crackled under the tires. It was deserted back there. The old wharf looked like it couldn't hold people. Its graying wood stood splintering in the darkness. The sky was becoming pale in the east. They both got out of the car and faced that direction.

"Everything is so quiet and peaceful. I've never watched the sun come up in the morning. My mind is always filled with so many other things."

Remy studied her closely. His hand found hers and clasped it. He pulled her to him in one fluid motion. His arms were around the small of her back. He kissed her deeply and could feel her warmth against him as he caressed her smooth arms. The kiss was hot and it affected him deeply. He wanted to inhale her. She did not pull away from him as she had in the past. They kissed like this for quite awhile. When Sugar Doll looked up the sun had already risen. She felt the heat of the sun begin to warm her back"You'd better get me home. Big Ma will be worried." Sugar Doll said flustered.

Remy wanted to recapture the moment and grabbed her into his arms once again kissing her deeply, feeling his passion stirring for her. This time she did push him away.

He took the hint and went to open her door. He crossed to his side looking at her. She was beautiful. He drove the rest of the way to her house quietly with none of his usual quips or jokes. His heart felt a yearning for her that he had never experienced before and he wanted to feel it. He wanted to get inside of the feeling and be surrounded by it. He wanted this feeling to consume him and it did.

Sugar Doll felt the beauty of the moment and noticed the difference in Remy. He looked so serious now. She wanted to take his hand but was afraid that it would break the mood they had in the car. They arrived at Big Ma's thirty minutes later. He got out of the car and opened the passenger side door for her.

"Good night lovely." He said and kissed her slightly swollen lips gently. She returned the sweet kiss.

"Good night Remy, thanks for the ride." Sugar Doll said as she walked away from him. The warm of his touch still tingled her hand.

"We still have a date for Monday?" Remy called after her.

"We still have a date." Sugar Doll smiled that beautiful smile and walked up the steps of her grandmother's white and green baby doll house.

The drive home was a lesson in pleasure and torment for Remy. He knew that he would have to contend with Bertrand about Sugar Doll. But he knew in his heart of hearts that they could have something good. Remy thought of her lips and the way that she held him. She smelled of magnolia and jasmine. "How am I going to tell Bertrand?" He thought aloud to himself but he needn't have worried. Bertrand had other things on his mind.

Chapter Nine

Mona stood at the counter wiping down the glasses from the night before. The bar was quiet and dark although it was bright and sunny outside. All of the wooden shutters were closed tight. She was ready to scream. Mona had a famous temper but nothing had made her angrier than what Tony had just told her. "That little heifer thinks that she's better than me? I am the one who paid for all of those fancy clothes she wears. I am the one who sent her to the best private schools."

Tony put his arms up in surrender. "I know sweetheart, but you know you haven't been around. She feels like you abandoned her." He stepped back from the bar just in case a flying glass would come his way. It didn't.

"She's not a child any more; she is twenty-one years old and should know better. Didn't I send a check every month to her grandmother? I was only eighteen years old when I had her that ungrateful bitch." As Mona put the glass down on the bar shelf it cracked. Disgusted she threw it into the garbage can.

"Of course you are right. But you know you could make the first move and go to see her sing. I can mind the bar while you are gone honey." Tony gave a placating look.

"I'm not going crawling to her. If it weren't for me she wouldn't even be on this earth. She gives me no credit at all and it hurts Tony, it hurts." Mona had tears in her eyes, a very unusual event.

Tony was moved and stood up to go to Mona and hold her. She accepted his affection. It was nice since it had been months since they had touched each other. There was no real reason except that the passion was just too strong and the fights were their undoing.

"You always make me feel good honey." Mona purred.

"I can make you feel better." Tony smiled his blue eyes flashing with desire. That was all it took for the two of them to be off and running.

Kevin leaned back on his chair musing about his friend's problem. He considered himself a magician in terms of getting away with crime. "So let me get this straight, you gamble in Biloxi, lose all of your money and then you contact Marsalas's camp for more money which you continue to lose"? Kevin asked

"Yeah and it's compounding daily." Bertrand said the sweat popping off of the side of his face.

"Man you are a trip"! Kevin exclaimed.

"Tell me something I don't know." Bertrand sighed.

"So now instead of repayment they are threatening to take over your club." Kevin took a drink of his beer.

"Man, help me. Tell me what to do!"! Bertrand almost cried.

"I suppose not, gambling never occurred to you." Kevin joked.

"Niggah I'm in trouble I'll quit for sure. Bertrand cried.

"All right, all right. Let me think. Did they give you a deadline"? Kevin asked.

"Next Friday."

"Damn!" Kevin stood up and circled his tiny room. The green paint was peeling and the once white ceiling was brown.

"All right, let me put my ear to the ground and find out how I can help you." Kevin looked out of the window at the causeway bridge that ran past his home on its way to cross the Mississippi River.

Remy sat watching CNN; there was a storm in the Gulf of Mexico. The wooden faced anchorman's blue eyes matched the color of his suit, "Hurricane Katrina promises to be a category five hurricane. Residents of lower Plaquemines Parish are being told to evacuate". Remy sat bolt upright in his chair. "Sugar Doll" he whispered under his breath. Big Ma didn't have a car. Bertrand had been their sole source of transportation and he hadn't seen him in about five days. Remy picked up the phone only to get a recording, "We're sorry all circuits are busy, please hang up the phone and try again later." Remy hung up and hit speed dial only to get the same recording. Feeling unproductive he thought to himself, "It probably won't hit anyway." He couldn't help feeling the knot in his stomach; he had a bad feeling about it.

He walked over to the window and peered out to see the usual view of the river and the trolley train. Even from this distance he could see that the water was choppy. Living on the third floor walkup of his tiny French Quarter apartment had its advantages. He saw the New Orleans ferry boat moored at the dock rollicking with the waves but obviously out of service. The sky was purple and gray and the clouds were fat with rain. This was nothing new in the city. Instead of the Crescent City they should call it the rainy city.

Remy had two gigs tonight. One was scheduled at Beauchamp's and the other at Mona's. He needed the money. He needed a new car. He picked up the phone to hit redial but he got the same message so he hung up and decided to get dressed for his gig. He pulled out his favorite black suit but his mind kept going to Sugar Doll. "She'll probably come to the French Quarter tonight. With all of their smooching he'd neglected to ask if she planned to come to town to perform. He knew that inviting her to Mona's was a foolish proposition. He found it hard to believe that Mona was the mother of this sweet, delicate creature. Mona was as beautiful as her daughter but she had a cruel streak about her and she was all business, all the time.

Remy descended the steps of his third floor apartment. The sweet smell of mold and hundred years of decay reached his nostrils. In order to live in the Quarters one had to live with the fact that the buildings were incredibly antiquated. He reached the second landing and stopped. He felt inexplicably uneasy. He knew that there was a problem and he needed to be the one to solve it. He hurried down the rest of the steps at a faster clip taking two at a time.

He reached Mona's at six o'clock and even with a heavy rain falling the French Quarters were packed with tourists and drunks. Some were walking out in the open while others stayed under the awnings of the businesses. A few fools were talking about throwing a hurricane party. He'd been to one while he was in college. It was fun and no danger as the hurricane hit its favorite town Greenville, Texas. Remy worked his way through the crowd and turned right onto the Rue St. Peter. Mona's loomed in the distance which was a stone's throw from the red light district.

Mona's clientele were always high class or mobsters. Some would say that they were one and the same. Politicians, celebrities and wealthy patrons hobnobbed at this high classed joint. The food was superb Louisiana cuisine. Remy needed the exposure and the extra cash. Tony had approached and even though he knew what the guy stood for the gig was double what he made at Beauchamp's.

He opened his flip phone and tried Sugar Doll's number and instead of a recording, he got a busy signal. He wished he would have talked to Bertrand or at least had Sugar Doll's cell phone number. He searched his phone in vain hoping that he had actually put in the number but had forgotten. "No such luck" he sighed. "She may already be evacuating." He thought hopefully. Even if the hurricane didn't hit the lower end of the parish may endure heavy flooding. Remy walked into the crowded restaurant. This was surprising considering the fact that the hurricane warnings had been very stern. Tony waved him over to the bar.

The man was always well dressed. Tony always wore expensive suits made of silk or fine linen. He stood against the bar wearing a classy gray suit which was obviously tailored. His striking blue eyes flashed with wit and charm. "It's hard to believe that this guy had ever been a gangster." Remy thought to himself and he shook Tony's hand.

"Hey Remy are you ready for tonight?" Tony asked smiling at the brisk business he saw before him. "Look at them, even with a hurricane they come out and I've got to take their money." Tony laughed. Remy laughed with him but wasn't as amused as he pretended. Tony was a smooth guy and that made him hard to trust.

"I'm ready, but are they?" Remy responded and looked out at the crowd. "I'm gonna stir up a hurricane tonight yeah!" He said in his Cajun brogue.

"Good attitude son." Tony said.

"How come ya'll booked me for a swanky joint like this?" Tony asked.

"Well to be honest with you, we are trying to attract a younger audience and you are really popular with the young girls and they bring in the fellas, you know what I mean?" Tony winked and smiled. Remy shook his head in acknowledgement. His father always told him to never ever trust a man who said, "to be honest with you", because that was the last thing that he was doing. Remy smiled at the memory of his father describing a polecat. His mind distracted by thoughts about Sugar Doll.

"Listen Tony, I've got a bad feeling about the hurricane. I'm friends with Sugar Doll and I can't get in touch with her. Bertrand's nowhere to be found and he is her usual ride. Do you know if Mona called her mother?" Remy looked hopefully at Tony.

Tony studied the handsome boy thoughtfully. "You are more than good friends with her, right?" Tony asked knowingly.

"Well yes, I mean no, I like her but that's about the length of it." Remy said.

"Wait right here my boy." Tony went behind the bar and through a side door which opened out into their upstairs apartments. He walked into the lavender bedroom he shared with

Mona. She lay asleep on the bed. "Baby, Baby, wake up." Tony nudged her gently.

"What?" Mona answered sleepily into her pillow.

"Have you checked on your mother?" Tony asked.

"Why?" Still half asleep Mona began to rouse herself up.

"There's a category five hurricane headed for the Gulf of Mexico. It looks like your Parish is right in its path. They are evacuating the Parish."

"Bertrand." Mona whispered as she sat up in the bed.

"He's nowhere to be found." Tony said.

"How do you know? Maybe he went to pick them up already." Mona yawned getting out of the bed and slipping on her slippers.

"Remy says he hasn't seen Bertrand in over five days." Tony said.

This drove Mona into action. She found her robe and went to her vanity table. She picked up the phone to call her mother. Tony knew then that he was no longer needed so he left the room as quietly as he had come. He did not envy Bertrand in that moment. He knew that there would be hell to pay. As he descended the stairs he hoped that Mona would get in contact with her mother. Even though the woman despised him and his "living in sin" with her daughter he knew her to be an honorable woman.

Tony returned to the bar and poured himself a drink. Remy still sat at the edge of the bar where he had left him. "Hey Remy, what you drinking?"

"I'll take a shot of Southern Comfort." Remy replied.

"Southern Comfort it is, one finger or two?" Tony asked as he took out a shot glass and a bottle of the liquor.

"One man, I've got to perform tonight." Tony poured the drink and handed it to Remy.

"Any news on Sugar Doll?" Remy asked hopefully.

"No but Mona is on the case." Tony said confidently. "That woman can work miracles." He smiled more to himself. The men toasted. "To miracles." They both said in unison. The rain outside was coming down harder. The streets were emptying.

"Sometimes rain is like poetry. It's so beautiful that you do not think of the damage it can cause." Remy drank his whiskey feeling its burn in his chest.

"Spoken like a true artist." Tony said.

"What time do I go on?" asked Remy.

"8 p.m. sharp." Tony said as he poured another drink.

"Do you really think that the hurricane will hit here?" Remy asked.

"Not likely and even if it does the French Quarters are set on higher ground and will be protected. This son is the center of New Orleans. Besides the city pumps will get rid of the excess water. I don't feel as positive for lower Plaquemines Parish however. That little slice of heaven should have disappeared long ago. Hurricanes Betsey and Camille should have taken it down but now forty years later it's time is at hand. Katrina may hit Florida or Texas instead. That's what happened in the past. I think you are worrying over nothing. That's what I think." Tony poured himself another drink.

"Why do you think that Plaquemines should have disappeared already?" Remy asked interested.

"Because it's so far below sea level that it is little more than marsh land." Answered Tony.

"God, I hope that they get out!" exclaimed Remy.

"Don't worry boy, everybody down there knows everyone else. Big Ma is no shrinking violet and she is kin to half the parish. I wouldn't be surprised if she was the first one out dragging Sugar Doll with her." Tony smiled encouragingly. Remy smiled back but he could not help but worry.

Chapter Ten

The rain plopped warmly onto Sugar Doll's back. She had managed to get all of the photo albums into two large pillow-cases. She had one garbage bag filled with warm, dry clothes. This was the poor man's suitcase. Big Ma had a bag filled with canned food, water, her strongbox and her medications all in clear sandwich baggies. They had tried to reach Bertrand in vain. The pastor of Big Ma's church had come by in his loaded van to try to squeeze them in but there was not enough room for them both. The pastor said that he would tell the sheriff to come by the house and escort them both to a storm shelter.

There were buses in Belle Chasse which were taking people to New Orleans or to Baton Rouge. Sugar Doll felt afraid, "Pastor Han, you know Big Ma is ill and I really don't want her going to some shelter. Would you please take her with you and I will pay whatever it costs at a hotel." She asked pleadingly. A bright streak of lightening flashed across the sky. The storm was getting worse. The rain outside came down on the tin roof like bullets. Pastor Han wiped his forehead with a kerchief, "My girl of course we can take Sister Evangeline with us."

Sugar Doll opened her purse and took out the five hundred dollars she had taken out of her bank account the day before after having waited in line for an hour. Pastor Han waved her off. "Sister, keep your money, you will probably need it. We don't know if it's God's plan for this hurricane to hit or not but all of us should be prepared. We will take care of the Sister." He said speaking in his best pastor's voice.

Big Ma looked worried. "I don't want to leave you down here by yourself." Big Ma cried. The horn of the van registered a sound. Sugar Doll looked out of the window to see young Brian, the pastor's son tooting the horn.

"I'm sorry about that but unfortunately my young son is right. We have a long trip ahead of us. We are going to Alexandria and the freeways are already getting clogged up, the official evacuation hasn't happened yet but in about two days it will and we want to be close to our destination." Pastor Han took another swipe at his beading forehead. It was warm but not as hot as his perspiring made it seem.

"Big Ma, please go. I promise to find you. I'll be all right. Bertrand is probably on his way down already." Sugar Doll took two hundred dollars and put into her grandmother's hand. "I'll see you in a couple of days." She said.

"All right, my blood pressure is already high so I'll go but I want to hear from you. I have this here cell phone and I expect you to call me as soon as you are away from trouble." Big Ma grabbed Sugar Doll and hugged her hard. "I love you child."

"I love you too Big Ma. Don't forget to take your medicine." Sugar Doll said tearing up in spite of herself. "I'll stay right here on the porch until someone stops to get me, either the sheriff or Bertrand." Sugar Doll smiled and kissed Big Ma on the forehead.

As they packed in the rest of Big Ma's belongings and made room for her in the church van Sugar Doll felt a sense of loss but she knew that she was just feeling sad. She waved goodbye as they pulled onto the shelled lane and hit the highway going much faster than she would expect from the Pastor.

She went back to the porch to sit in the rocking chair most occupied by her grandmother. The rain splashed from the porch banister and splattered a little on her face. She watched the waving cat tails all beige and fuzzy across the street. The rain looked like sheets of glass coming down. The neighborhood was quiet. The next door neighbors had already been on vacation in Mississippi so she could only assume that they would weather the storm there. She fell asleep from the lull of the rain. A powerful thunder boom woke her from her sleep. She sat up disoriented. The sky had turned almost black although it was one o'clock in the afternoon. She got up and walked through the house to the back porch to look out at the levee. She could make out a funnel cloud which was touching down on the river. She'd seen these before and they rarely came off of the water. Her grandfather used to call them the finger of God. She stood in awe for awhile.

She went back into the living room and tried the television. It came on with news about the hurricane's progress. She was relieved that there was still electricity. The newscaster showed a graphic of the path of the hurricane and she could see that the hurricane was headed directly for her tiny peninsula. "Mandatory evacuations have been ordered for lower Plaquemines Parish and surrounding areas." For the first time Sugar Doll felt scared. Just then a white Parish police car pulled into the driveway flashing its blue lights.

The officer driving got out of his car in the pouring rain and ran toward the house. "Ma'am do you have transportation to a safe area?" the officer asked.

"No sir, I don't. My Pastor said that he would notify the police. Are you here to collect me?" Sugar Doll asked.

"We did receive the call but I'm calling on residents to evacuate. The buses in Belle Chasse are filling up quickly. I will drive you as far as that and then you can get transport from there." he said.

"Thank you, Officer Benson." Sugar Doll said reading his name plate.

"You are welcome, gather up your things and I'll pull the car closer to the house." He said and ran back outside. The lights of his car were still flashing. Sugar Doll felt relief. She had only two suitcases as she had put the photo albums in the van with the Pastor. The car pulled up as Sugar Doll locked the front door to the house. As they drove away onto the highway she looked back over her shoulder at the green and white house she had grown up in and felt a rush of sadness. She hoped that she would find it there again safe and sound. The lightening and thunder became more violent as they drove up the highway.

Miles away from Sugar Doll's escape, Bertrand tried for the fourth time to break through the busy circuits. He finally got a ring which had a strange echo to it. The phone rang and rang but he was afraid to hang up. He knew that Big Ma and Sugar Doll needed him and here he was holed up in a motel with Kevin. Finally when he realized that he wasn't making any progress he hung up the phone.

"Man I gotta go down to the country to get Big Ma and Sugar Doll. That hurricane is going to hit for sure." Bertrand said to Kevin who was relaxing on the other bed in the room watching the news on mute.

"Niggah what are you talking about? Tonight is the night." Kevin said aggravated.

"A hurricane coming bro and I can't just leave them with no help. Our cousins aren't down there so that leaves me." Bertrand said getting up and looking for his car keys."

"Man, that storm ain't gonna touch ground for at least two more days. We got time, plus traffic is going to be ridiculous. It's probably not even going to come close to us. It's going where it always goes, Greenville, Texas." Kevin broke into a grin.

"Oh, so now you a weatherman? Looka here man, I'm going that's all." Bertrand headed for the door.

"At least call before you go, they may have already left and you all set to go down there for nothing." Kevin admonished.

"I did call several times but no one answered the one time I got a line. Other times the circuits are busy." Bertrand said.

"So you see there, if I know Big Ma like I think I know her they have hauled ass about three days ago and you know it." Kevin stood up and walked to Bertrand.

"Hey, doesn't Sugar Doll have a cell phone? Sometimes they are not affected by busy circuits." Kevin suggested.

"Yeah, I have it here, or is this Big Ma's number?" Bertrand shrugged and dialed the number. Big Ma answered on the second ring.

"Hey, where are you now?" Big Ma asked thinking that it was Sugar Doll.

"I'm in Baton Rouge, where are you"? Bertrand asked.

"Who is this?" Big Ma asked confused.

"It's Bertrand. Did you and Sugar Doll get out of the parish?" Bertrand asked as Kevin returned to his comfortable spot on the bed.

"No, I'm here with Pastor Han on our way to Alexandria but there wasn't enough room for Sugar Doll. She was waiting for you to come or call and now here you are in Baton Rouge." Big Ma sighed.

"I'm going to get her right now." Bertrand felt his heart tighten in his chest.

"No you ain't, I sent the sheriff to go and get her so Lawd knows where she is now. You go and find out what shelter she is in and then take her back to Baton Rouge with you. We can all meet up after the storm." Big Ma said goodbye wanting to keep the phone open for Sugar Doll's call. She didn't know how to work the caller id portion of the phone. It confused her. She looked out the back van window in prayer, "Lawd, Lawd keep my granddaughter safe."

The warmth of the police car was a drastic difference from the cold rain droplets which pelted Sugar Doll as the officer let her off in front of Belle Chasse High School. She shivered as she got out of the car. The change in temperature was probably due to the rise in pressure from the storm. There were people sitting in corners of the school gymnasium awaiting buses to evacuate them to safer areas. Sugar Doll sat down in the middle of the gymnasium floor. She gazed mournfully at the basket. This was a far cry from all of those school basketball games they had attended at their rival school.

"Sugar Doll?" An unmistakable voice rang out as Patrice an old high school buddy ran over to her. "Girl I thought that was you." Patrice hugged Sugar Doll's shoulders from behind. Sugar Doll felt so happy to see someone she knew that she cried.

"Girl, now don't you cry, me and my sister think that they done forgot about us honey. We are thinking of just driving to the city and going to the Superdome in New Orleans to sit this storm out." Patrice smiled.

"I thought the buses were taking everyone to Baton Rouge?" Sugar Doll asked surprised.

"Yeah, some of them are but they fill up quickly and I don't think that they are coming back for us anytime soon. You can come with my sister Elise and me if you want to, we got room. We'll ride this storm out and then go party in the French Quarters girl. You sing there I heard?"

"Yes I do." Sugar Doll thought of Remy then and shook her head in agreement. She needed to see him, to hold him, to feel safe. Patrice gave her friend a hand to get up.

"C'mon girl let's go before the storm gets worse. We don't want to weather the storm in Belle Chasse." The girls walked arm in arm over to a very obese young woman who unfortunately was eating a donut. "Elise, where did you get that donut?" You know you ain't supposed to be eating no high caloric content." Patrice scolded.

"A priest gave it to me. I couldn't say no." Elise shrugged.

"Why not? We ain't Catholic! If your big ass catch a heart attack and die you'll be right there at a Baptist church." Patrice picked up her sister's bags. Let's go. You so lucky momma not alive to see you like this. Wipe them crumbs from your face and you'd better not cry." Patrice hugged what she could of her enormous sister.

Patrice decided to park her car in the French Quarters because of the traffic and the higher level of ground. They walked the several blocks holding onto each other. Sugar Doll looked around several times hoping to see Remy. A heat of regret rose up in her cheeks. She knew that he was at Mona's club. She almost wished that she weren't so stubborn. Patrice was dragging her along by the arm. Sugar Doll felt compelled to keep walking at the fast pace. The rain and the rising water created a sense of urgency. Elise was surprisingly quick given her enormous girth. She moved like a cat under the pressure of the heavy rain. The umbrella they shared was blown forward by a strong gust of wind. The spokes stretched outward. Elise looked up at the umbrella as though it had betrayed her. Finally the Superdome was in sight. On many occasions they had made this same trek but it didn't take half as long and even the rain was softer, quieter back then. This rain pelted the girls on the face, raining down like tiny pins set to kill them slowly. The girls arrived at the Superdome in pouring rain. The streets were beginning to flood. The water sloshed around their ankles.

An old man stood in front of one of the glass doors. He stopped them, "The Red Cross is giving out blankets and food. Ya'll go get ya'll some before they run out."

"Thanks baby." Elise bustled to the door. Such was the kindness of old men in New Orleans they always wanted to help someone. Sugar Doll wondered if he had a blanket and food. She looked at him over her shoulder. He leaned against the door seeming to wait for others to tell them this news. Sugar Doll thought of her grandfather then, long since dead. He was as light as a white man but he preached in the Baptist church with a deep roll of a voice. She'd been frightened of him. He had been kind to her. So kind that she called him daddy along with her aunts and uncles because her daddy had long since died and she didn't know any better.

On the streets during their run there seemed only scattered people walking about only a few or so but as soon as they entered the Superdome the mass of humanity was palpable. It was unusually hot in the dome considering the coldness of the rain. There was no heating system either. It was the many people who had come here smelling of mud, of hair grease, of baby powder who made up the crowds. Sugar Doll looked around at the packed Superdome. She knew that none of her relatives were there. These were the locals. She felt out of place. A country girl in the big city.

People sat amongst their families, waiting expectantly looking at the top of the dome and the trickle of water that was falling through the cracks. The spirit seemed relaxed. No one really thought that the hurricane would actually hit the city. Everyone talked about how they were going home to cook some red beans or fry some catfish. The spirit was "jovial" the word came to Sugar Doll. Like this was an outing they could talk about the next day. Everyone had the New Orleans spirit, laughing and joking with each other.

As they climbed the steps of the stadium Patrice saw a family "from down home" and ran off toward them. Sugar Doll didn't look for Reverend Han or Big Ma because she knew that they were headed up north away from the water and trouble in general. She imagined that she was in the van with them smelling that strong coffee Big Ma had brewed for the car and the spearmint gum that inevitably followed.

The heat of the Superdome rose to greet them the higher they climbed up the steep stairs. Elise tugged at her sleeve. "Sugar Doll girl I've been calling you for a minute. C'mon Patrice has gotten us a nice spot." Sugar Doll turned around and slowly followed her friend. She realized that she didn't want to be there. She thought of Remy. As she followed Elise she realized that she wanted to return to the French Quarter. It seemed safer there, calmer, more familiar. She didn't want to remain in this stuffy building.

She had only been to the Superdome once for the Bayou Classic. The crowd was thick as it was on this day but the air conditioners were on full tilt. As they descended the stairs she looked over and saw a few young boys' playing cards rather excitedly. "Man you cheat!" One argued but his smile betrayed him.

"Naw man, c'mon now!" the other young boy exclaimed. Elise stopped to look at the game. "Ya'll both cheat!" She giggled flirting. The boys looked up playfully. One was a deep brown complexion. He smiled beautifully at Elise.

"You want to play?" He asked.

"No I don't play with strangers." Elise stopped flattered by the offer.

"My name's Tommy, what's yours and your friend's?" He cast longing eyes up at Sugar Doll. Elise understood the look and her smile immediately faded.

"I'm Elise, her name is Sugar Doll." Her giggling gone she stepped to the side almost pushing Sugar Doll in front of her large body as though she wanted to hide.

"Well hello Sugar Doll!" Tommy exclaimed in a growling voice. His friend stood up by his side.

"I'm Bobby Joe" the darker skinned boy stammered. They both were about 15 years old more or less. Little boys in her eyes but then she did look young for twenty-one.

Sugar Doll smiled at them but turned to Elise, "Listen, I've got to go, my mother's place is in the French Quarters. I think I'll ride the storm out there."

Elise immediately brightened. "Okay" she turned toward the boys to continue their conversation but their smiles had turned into concern.

"C'mon girl" Tommy said exasperated. "It's dangerous out there, that storm ain't no joke." Bobby Joe chimed in also expressing concern. They looked at each other amazed that they'd spoken in unison. They returned their attention to Sugar Doll not giving in to their usual high fives or joking.

"If she want to go, let her go." Elise spoke up defensively.

"Damn girl, I thought she was your friend! A hurricane ain't nothing to play with!" Tommy exclaimed.

Elise cringed, "My name is Elise!" She looked as though she were going to cry. Patrice arrived walking up the stairs. "What's taking ya'll so damned long? I'm trying to save us a spot."

"Sugar Doll wants to go back to the Quarters," Elise spat out. Sugar Doll began descending the stairs calmly. Patrice grabbed her arm, "Girl you crazy, you saw the weather out there. It's probably gotten worse."

"I'll be all right." Sugar Doll said feeling a bit unsure of her resolve but more determined to go than ever. She needed to see Remy, to hold him. She opened her cell phone and rang him.

"This is Remy, leave a message dahling." His heavy drawl crawled through the phone and touched her. She could feel his kiss on her lips. "Remy, I'm at the Superdome; I want to come to Mona's to ride out the hurricane. Call me when you get this message. Oh and break a leg!" Sugar Doll hung up and tried to smile but she looked up at the ceiling and saw rain dripping through the roof.

As she continued to descend she felt a warm hand grab her shoulder, "Girl don't go out there. It could be dangerous too. The city is emptying out and all that's left is the worst sorts of people who are looking to rob and steal and who knows what all else?"

Tommy pleaded with Sugar Doll. "If you were my sister I wouldn't let you go." Tommy's eyes were kind.

She turned full around to see a repentant Elise, Patrice, Tommy and Bobby Joe all looking like a makeshift choir. It made her smile.

"I'll be all right; my boyfriend is in the Quarter. He is going to meet me." She waved goodbye and trotted off leaving the choir of friends staring helplessly after her.

As she waded through the mass of humanity who were all vying to get a place in the stadium she felt that she had made the right decision. Something wasn't right. People seemed too desperate and too unprepared. As she stepped under the awning of the dome the force of the rain hit her. It was strong but she was determined. She spotted an old tarp that looked like it had been blown against the building. She grabbed it and wrapped it around her entire body. She took off the belt on her jeans and wrapped it around her waist and felt pleased with her ingenuity. "Mother necessity where would we be?" She sang the tune from an old cartoon. "Well here goes," she thought as she stepped into the strong wind. The water was up to her knee caps now and she felt afraid but certain that the hurricane had not hit ground yet. She had time, time to see Remy.

Chapter Eleven

Bertrand loaded his gun. It felt unusual in his hands. He had only purchased it for protection against robbers. "Now here I am the robber," he thought to himself. He looked down at the ski mask and thought how stupid it was to go shopping for an item like this in the hottest city on the planet. He had suggested simple pantyhose but Kevin had reasoned with him that these were easy to see through. What would his father the deacon think? "Son, thieving and robbing and lying and cheating all in the same category with God. Don't even think about killing. Never point a gun at a man if you don't intend to use it because if you miss or threaten he's coming for you." That's all his father had told him about a life of crime. Up till now he'd avoided it. Gambling wasn't crime as far as he was concerned but then the debt kept growing. He was a big man and hiding out wasn't an option. "I just don't want to lose my bar. I'm sorry daddy." Bertrand whispered to himself like a prayer. He loaded the gun and walked to the garage. He rationalized that his father didn't agree with his lifestyle anyway. He wanted him to work in a church. "A fool's game," Bertrand sighed aloud. A cold trickle of sweat rolled down his back. A scripture came to him, "The fool says in his mind there is no

God." He would have considered it an omen but decided that it was just his Baptist mind going wild with thoughts of sin.

Kevin waited in the car. The fresh smell of French fries wafted up from the window. Kevin sat there munching. He handed up a bag of Burger King to Bertrand. "Eat like a king brother because tonight we are going to be rich." Bertrand grabbed the bag and then opened the door. He slid in easily onto the soft leather interior of his Lincoln Continental.

"Hey man, you ready for tonight?" Kevin asked between bites. Bertrand looked down at the bag. He didn't feel like a King. "Come on man, eat. We need to go over the plan again. I know your big ass is hungry." Bertrand agreed and opened the bag and looked disappointedly at Kevin.

"What's wrong? A Whopper, right, extra cheese?" Kevin asked.

"I'm a big man, I meant two of those." Bertrand said.

"When you mean two, then you say two." Kevin opened his whooper and began casually eating it.

"All right man, so what's the plan?" Bertrand asked munching his fries.

"The plan is still the same. You go into that back hallway. I'll follow you then we walk in and bust up the game. We hold Marsalas hostage so to speak and his boys. Then we get the money." Kevin and Bertrand clinked fists like a toast.

"It's so simple man. No one would ever think to rob the robber." Bertrand chuckled.

"Yeah like Robin Hood, 'cept we is keeping the money." Kevin laughed.

Bertrand thought about tonight and he felt a moment of dread. He began to sweat again. "Kevin, what if we get caught?" he asked.

"We ain't gonna get caught. We are going to catch them off guard. As far as they know with this hurricane nobody is even thinking about them."

Bertrand smiled slightly reassured as he heard the pounding rain outside. He felt scared but all of his thoughts of God and goodness disappeared like the wind.

~

Sugar Doll began to see the wisdom of her friend's words. As she struggled against the wind it was a constant battle to make it across the street. She saw people running haphazardly to and fro. She alone looked like she had a direction, a focus. She thought of a song Remy sang to her one night. She imagined his face and was even more determined to press onward. The pelts of the rain fell steadily like bullets. They showered down on her. As she passed the Riverwalk she looked between the buildings and saw the waves crashing up against the banks. It was scary to see it. The rain felt cold and she shivered and began to run in earnest. There were smatterings of people headed in the opposite direction but no signs telling her that she was going the wrong way. She approached St. Peter's street. As she looked down the long Tchopotulis Avenue she saw hundreds of cars bumper to bumper, headed for the Mississippi River Bridge which was right up over her head. She looked up into the big droplets of rain and saw the cars cramming so close to each other that they looked like one giant organism.

This rush to leave was commonplace in lower Plaquemines Parish where just the slightest tropical storm could send hordes of trailer park dwellers packing due to intense flooding. This, however, never occurred in New Orleans Proper which was so famous that even God had stopped his mighty winds and flooding for 40 years. The city was where people usually ran to have hurricane parties and such.

A sign flew past Sugar Doll. Its metal yellow corners hit the side of a brick building and took a chunk off with it. "That could have been my face." Sugar Doll thought absently touching her face to make sure that it was still there. For the first time Sugar Doll felt real fear. She ran faster, picking up the pace. She heated up under the makeshift tarp she had wrapped around her waist. The French Quarters lay ahead as she turned past St. Louis cathedral and shot down Royal. She saw two news trucks. The reporters were there in front of their cameras. They stood almost side by side even though the trucks identified two separate news agencies.

"Officials are saying, "Get out of town. This is not the storm to try to ride out people. You must leave now. People who insist on remaining are only placing themselves in danger." News reporter Jana Carlsbad wrapped up her broadcast.

"What the hell are we still doing here then?" She quipped to her cameraman Buddy who was turning off the equipment.

"Honey, we are making news." He joked back and gave her a wink.

"Where to next"? Jana asked.

"Well, we definitely need to get to higher ground, but I'm not a native. I think that St. Charles Avenue should be a good vantage point." The cameraman said distracted as he buckled his leather carrying case to secure his expensive camera.

"Shouldn't we go to the waterfront? Jana disagreed.

"We can capture the waves jumping up on the shore." She suggested.

"Everybody will be doing that." Buddy shrugged sarcastically.

"We'll find an empty spot. Perhaps across the river by Algiers. We can get the poor person's perspective." Jana smiled encouragingly. She headed for the truck.

"Who wants that?" Buddy asked.

"America." Jana yelled over her shoulder before she got into the car. "America."

Sugar Doll trotted past the news van without any questions or the usual interest that people normally display. Jana noticed the girl and automatically her reporter's mind began working. The girl was beautiful and young. She cut an intriguing figure running so alone in hurricane weather. "Where was she going? Would she survive the storm? Who was waiting for her?" These questions would remain with Jana for a lifetime. She just didn't know it in that moment. She thought of getting a photo of the girl but it was too late and too wet. Jana climbed into the truck, she had work to do.

Bertrand strapped himself in for the ride of his life. The rain was coming down harder now. Visibility on the road was very low. There were many cars coming from the opposite direction. Many people were trying to get out of town and here they were trying to get into the city. They were trying to get into mischief. Kevin seemed unconcerned about the mass exodus they were witnessing. The bridge over Lake Ponchartrain, which seemed sturdy but the water below was choppy and waves lapped at the bridge. It was a long stretch between Baton Rouge and New Orleans.

"Hey man, I can swim good and all but I'm scared I won't be able to fight off these waves." Bertrand said nervously.

"Don't look at the water. Just keep your eyes straight ahead. That's what I'm doing." Kevin said reassuringly.

"Man we are surrounded by water. How can you act like you don't see it?" Bertrand began to sweat.

"Calm down man, are we going to do this or not? We ain't got time for you to be freaking out now. We are an hour away from easy money." Kevin smiled at him.

"Ain't no such thing as easy money." Bertrand countered.

"Are you changing your mind man? I could have let someone else in on this but I chose your big ass because you in trouble. Look we get in and we get out and we spend the money. We ain't robbing a bank. We robbing a gangster. They ain't gonna report it to the police. They ain't gonna do nothing but give us that money." Kevin adjusted his cap.

"You think they aren't going to come after us bro?" Bertrand asked, the thought occurring to him for the first time.

"No, they ain't gonna come after us. We are going to disappear into the hurricane man. It's like God wants us to have this money. I didn't plan for the storm but look, here it is." Kevin pointed at the darkening skies and the purple clouds fat with rain.

"That's true." Bertrand conceded.

"It sure is true. You God damned right its true. They are going to think that we are just some desperate niggers from the 9th Ward and they are going to leave us alone. You Dig?" Kevin laughed.

"I can DIG it." Bertrand laughed at the old expression.

Sugar Doll finally stood in front of the club. Her mother's place. She'd dreaded going there. There was music playing and people eating. It didn't match the desertion and desperation she'd just left behind her. She untied her tarp and cast it aside. She walked down the alleyway to the side of the building. She didn't want to go in the front dressed as she was. As she walked into the kitchen she saw the cooks and dishwasher all huddled around the radio. The announcer was tracking the storm and warning the people of New Orleans to get out.

"Ron, man we need to get the hell out of here. I have to go across the river and get my family. We don't have a car." One of the young men said.

"They have probably already left. Don't worry about them. The sheriff will get them out. We are on higher ground here. The Quarter ain't in no danger." Ron said, "Now ya'll get back to work or Miss Mona will have all of our asses." He waved to everyone. They turned to see Sugar Doll standing there.

"Why if I never, this here is Miss Mona's daughter." Ron said loudly.

Sugar Doll didn't recognize any of these men. She just waved and walked past them.

"I didn't know that Miss Mona had a daughter but she sure do look like her." The younger man said. "She sure do look like the best of her!"

"She got a picture of her on her desk." Ron supplied.

Sugar Doll left the men to talk as she entered the club. She was relieved to see Remy and Tony sitting at the bar. They didn't see her.

She walked up behind Remy and tapped his shoulder.

He turned around and let out a whoop when he saw her.

"Now, what are you doing here? I thought that you were still down in the country stranded or something. Did Bertrand come to get you after all?" Remy asked.

"No, I haven't seen Bertrand in a while. I don't know what happened to him." Sugar Doll answered.

"What about Big Ma?" Remy asked concerned.

"Pastor Han picked her up. They sent the sheriff for me and then I ran into some old high school buddies but I left them at the Superdome to come here." Sugar Doll caught him up on her adventures. Now that they were spoken aloud they didn't seem so harrowing.

"You mean to tell me that you walked all the way from the Superdome by yourself?" Remy asked angrily.

"That was dangerous kid." Tony chimed in as he sat there sipping his scotch.

"No one bothered me. Everyone is trying to get out of town, everyone but ya'll."

"We've got time kid. Hurricanes are the only type of natural disaster in which you have loads of time to pack up and get out. I'm packed already but I'm not leaving until they tell me I have to leave." Tony said confidently.

Remy stood and offered Sugar Doll his seat.

"I'm going on in a minute. I'm glad that you are here Sugar." Remy kissed her cheek and prepared to go onstage.

"You'd better go and tell your mother you are here. She's got the New Orleans police on the lookout and she will beat down the parish to get to you. She's upstairs in her room." Tony offered.

Sugar Doll followed the walkway along the bar and went up the stairs to her mother's private rooms. She'd only been there once before but she remembered the room and the curving stairway. She knocked timidly on the door. She walked in to see her mother pacing back and forth on the phone but obviously talking to herself.

"These damned circuits, what in the hell is going on here?" She slammed down the phone for the fifth time but this time when she looked up Sugar Doll stood before her.

Uncharacteristically she ran to her and grabbed her into her arms. "Oh honey, you are safe. Where is your grandmother?" Mona asked.

"Pastor Han picked her up this morning. There wasn't enough room for me so Big Ma sent the sheriff. He brought me to Belle Chasse and then I saw Patrice so we came up to the Superdome but it's hot and disgusting in there so I came up to the Quarters.

"How?" Mona asked.

"I walked." Sugar Doll answered.

"You walked that distance by yourself?" Mona was set to reprimand her but was too happy to do so. She settled down and gave Sugar Doll another hug.

"We still have to leave. After the show tonight we are going to close down and go up to Baton Rouge or Alexandria. Well away from the storm. Did you bring any clothes with you?"

"I left them all in Patrice's car but they are here in the Quarters." Sugar Doll said.

"No matter, we are about the same size, you can borrow some of my clothes." Mona was happy to being playing mother again.

"Your friend is singing tonight. Why don't you accompany him?" Mona suggested.

It seemed that Mona was getting her wish after all. Sugar Doll just decided to go with the flow.

"Why not? I'm here now." She conceded.

Mona gave a shriek of delight. She went to her closet and pulled out a beautiful gown for her daughter to wear.

The music downstairs began to play. Sugar Doll could hear wisps of Remy's voice floating up through the vent. She suddenly felt excited. She heard the storm outside but it was warm here. The storm was no longer within her but without and she felt at peace. Everything was as it should be.

Tony left the kid by the stage and went off to call Marsalas about the game. The game was just a front for the money laundering that he used the club for but it was a good time and the fellas enjoyed it. They even played sometimes into the night. It was profitable and entertaining. The hurricane had preempted their plans a bit so that not all of the major players were able to come into town but it was still going to be lucrative. The club was packed. He heard some of the customers say that this may be their last chance to eat a good meal at a fancy restaurant in the Quarters. Remy had pulled in a younger crowd and no one looked like they were really paying attention to the storm outside.

"Ladies and Gentlemen, we have a young man coming up to the stage that ya'll all are familiar with and he is something else." The crowd clapped and yelled loudly. .

"Mr. Remy Gaudeaux"! The announcer stood clapping. Remy mounted the stage and shook his hand vigorously. As the announcer left the stage he grabbed the microphone.

"Ya'll ready to whip up a hurricane?" Remy shouted to the already lively crowd.

"Yeah!" They responded. "Down home blues, Down home blues…" Remy began to croon and people began dancing between the tables.

The rain was hitting the building hard. The huge glass windows of the dinner club reflected the strong winds which were brewing outside. The rain was pelting sideways. A few customers close to the windows looked a little scared but then New Orleans was famous for summer storms and the Quarter was never really affected. A camera crew stood outside. Jana Carlsbad had heard the music as they were packing up and decided to direct the crew to this area.

"Can you believe people are partying? This is a Category 5 hurricane. What is wrong with these people?" Jana asked.

"Honey this is New Orleans. These people been through storms before cher." Randy the crew member was unpacking his gear. Buddy had left them after they'd shot the last footage.

"Well let's get some footage of this and then get the hell out of here. The storm is going to hit ground tomorrow morning." Jana said.

"Can I help ya'll?" The hostess asked practically barring the way into the club.

"Yes, I am Jana Carlsbad for News Scene 8 and I need to speak to the owner. I would like to shoot some footage of your little hurricane party." Jana extended her hand but the hostess ignored it. She picked up the phone to call Mona's private rooms. Mona picked up on the first ring. She'd been expecting the police to come and close them down.

"Miss Mona, there is a news crew here who wants to shoot some footage of your club." The hostess related.

Mona's heart soared. This could be very good for the club. "Let them in baby, I'll be down in a minute." Mona smiled at this unexpected opportunity.

"Sugar Doll, hurry up girl, you are going to be on the news!" Mona turned and patted powder on her face and straightened her wig.

There were some in the crowd who recognized Jana. She smiled and waved. "Continue having fun."

The crowd obliged. Remy was really swinging now. Sugar Doll entered the side door dressed in a beautiful floor length red gown with the back cut out and a red long scarf which draped around her neck. The look of the innocent girl was gone. She was beautiful and resplendent. The crowd closest to her let out an appreciative sigh. Remy turned to see her standing there. He stopped singing and beckoned her to the stage. Everybody put your hands together for "Sugar Doll"! The crowd went wild. Most of them didn't even know who this lovely woman was but they could tell that they were in for a treat.

"Roll camera." Jana said in the background.

"In the final moments of the evacuation we came upon this popular restaurant, Mona's. As you can see behind me the crowd seems unconcerned with the waves which are lapping at the Riverwalk less than a mile away. We are in the famous French Quarters and even though I am told this is not a hurricane party, it would be hard to think of it as anything else." Jana smiled and signaled the cameraman to film Sugar Doll and Remy onstage and the crowd's reactions.

Mona descended the steps and introduced herself to the reporter.

"Miss Mona, aren't you afraid of endangering the good folks who have come to your establishment on such a night?" Jana asked just as the cameraman swung the camera back to her.

"Well, these folks just want to have a good time. We haven't been asked by the sheriff's office to leave nor have we heard any evacuation sirens. I've been watching the news and that hasn't occurred yet." Mona said confidently.

"Actually there have been calls for mandatory evacuations." Jana corrected her.

"Well, most of these customers are regulars and they know the city. Some folks wait until the last possible moment to avoid traffic. I do that myself. We will be closed and boarded by midnight tonight." Mona smiled.

"There you have it. New Orleans, the land that time forgot. A little happiness in a desperate time. This is Jana Carlsbad reporting." The camera light stopped blinking.

"Let's go fellas. Traffic or not, I'm getting out of here." Jana headed for the door and Randy picked up his case and followed her. His things were atthe station.

Chapter Twelve

Bertrand and Kevin drove slowly through the Quarter. There were smatterings of people but it was eerily quiet.

"Hey man do you think that they will still do this tonight?" Bertrand asked.

"Yeah, they are crooks man, they got to get their money together and what better time to do it than when the cops are busy evacuating the parishes? Kevin smiled.

"That's true. Like us, they is shady." Bertrand quipped.

"We wait here until we see them arriving. I've staked out this spot. They won't see us but we sure can see them." Kevin smiled. He pulled out a flask with whiskey in it and took a swig. He handed it over to Bertrand who also took a swig.

Moments later, Tony came out of the side door. He glanced around and waved at someone who was not in their line of vision. A car pulled forward and someone got out of the car. The umbrella hid their identity.

Kevin elbowed Bertrand and the two waited and watched. Tony came out a total of five times. A half hour past with silence between the two men.

"What do we do now?" Bertrand asked.

"We wait." Kevin answered.

Sugar Doll couldn't believe the crowd and the harmony which she and Remy experienced together. After the set people started to leave. The storm outside had become undeniably wild and dangerous.

"Ladies and gentlemen, for your own safety we here at Mona's want to thank you for coming out but it's time now to pay respect to another lady, Hurricane Katrina. Ya'll be careful. You don't have to go home but you can't stay here. Have a good evening and a safe trip out of New Orleans proper. We'll be here when you come back!" The crowd clapped at this pronouncement and began to gather their things. The staff had already gone home or to storm shelters. The streets were filled with water and rain, which scattered past at a high rate of velocity.

"What are you going to do Remy?" Sugar Doll asked concerned.

"Well I'm gonna walk over to my apartments and pick up some things and then I'm going to head on up to Gonzales by my brother. Do you want to come with me?" Remy asked.

"Yes." Sugar Doll answered immediately. "Let me go and change." She kissed him on the cheek and headed for the stairs.

"You aren't going with that boy. You are coming with us where I can keep an eye on you. Your grandmother wouldn't like it." Mona said as she packed her bags.

"Well, I'm a grown woman and I can do what I want to do. I'll call you when I get there, it's right outside of your house in Baton Rouge anyway. I don't want to upset you but I want to go with him." Sugar Doll said.

Tony approached, "Let her go Mona. He's a good kid. He cares about her and will take good care of her. Let her go." He put his hand on her shoulder.

"Oh all right, but you'd better call me as soon as you get to where you are going and remember that even though the circuits are busy you can keep trying until you get through. Go pack up some of my clothes to wear. I'll see you in a few days." Mona smiled. She was happy that her daughter was actually responding to her so she didn't want to ruin the moment by insisting.

"Just like us." Tony said.

"Oh God I hope not." Mona said

The trees blew wildly back and forth in the increasing wind and rain. Remy looked up the staircase to see Sugar Doll descending with case in hand. His blue eyes flashed with desire. Warmth spread through Sugar Doll's body and their eyes met. She reached for his hand and they walked out into the pouring rain. The rain no longer felt cold and intimidating to Sugar Doll. It now felt warm and sensual.

"Let's go to my apartment to pick up a few things." Remy said into her ear. The warmth coursed through her body and her fingertips tingled. They ran hand in hand in the rain. As they approached Rue de la Decatur he led her around the corner to a narrow stairwell. Sugar Doll had never been to Remy's apartment. Her heart picked up its pace. As they walked up the stairway she felt nervous. Remy opened the door, "Welcome to my humble abode." He winked and held the door open for her to pass through. The apartment was cool and dark. The blinds were closed on the large windows which overlooked Tchopotulis Street. The air conditioner rumbled in the corner of the room from a third window which faced the street. The décor of the room was blue and green. There was a very masculine sense to it. The furnishings were subtle with modern lines. Sugar Doll looked around appreciatively. Remy had style. She had expected a stale smelling dormitory styled room with eclectic furniture but this had showroom quality.

"We've both had a trying day, let's have a drink." Remy went to a mahogany cabinet and pulled out a dark bottle of wine. Sugar Doll sat down on the plush forest green couch.

"This is a nice place you have here Remy. I'm impressed." Sugar Doll nodded. He walked over and handed her a drink. The rain outside became a downpour. Remy smiled easily, he could see that she was nervous.

"Relax Sugar; Gonzales is only a one hour drive from here in drive time tops. We'll be there in no time." Remy soothed her.

"It's not the weather that has me nervous Remy." She said shyly looking into his eyes. They were an interesting color of blue, turquoise really. "It's just all of the talk on the news and well…my mother that's got me nervous." Sugar Doll put down her drink. She could feel it warming her up in places she was unaccustomed to feeling.

"I understand, trust me, I've seen Mona in action, she can be pretty convincing." Remy smiled.

"Yes, I'm surprised by her warmth today. I'm also curious about why she's so interested in me all of a sudden. I've been singing at Beauchamp's for months now." Sugar Doll voiced what she had been thinking.

"I never hear you talk about it, shucks for awhile there I thought Big Ma was your mother." Remy joked.

"In a real way, she is." Sugar Doll said thoughtfully.

There was silence between them. Sugar Doll reached for her drink. Remy touched her arm and she returned the drink to the coffee table.

"I've been thinking about that night on the pier." He said his face becoming flushed.

"Me too." Sugar Doll sighed quickly.

"I wonder if..." Remy did not finish his sentence.

"If what?" Sugar Doll asked afraid of the answer.

"I don't really know how to say it." He answered looking away.

"If you made a mistake?" Sugar Doll asked a bit hurt by the thought.

"No, not exactly, but if we made a mistake. I think about you all the time girl."

"But Bertrand," he sputtered "And now your mother." He turned to face her.

"Oh," Sugar Doll said understanding. "Business." She said flatly rising suddenly.

Remy stood with her lightly grabbing her arm, "Not business, not business at all." He repeated softly.

"Then what?" Sugar Doll questioned anger rising up within her. Remy stepped closer to her and engulfed her in a kiss. The rain beat on the roof urgently. His tongue searched her mouth and his lips soft around hers were warm and pulsing. The rain was like music playing to their passion. As Sugar Doll gave into the kiss her body aching she realized that her question had not been answered. She would not give into him as much as she wanted to until she had the answer. She recovered herself and pulled away slightly not strong enough to break out of Remy's strong embrace. She felt his desire on her and it almost melted her resolve.

"Then what is it?" She asked him softly, urgently, passion pulsing through her body.

ↈ

"Monty, I'm glad you could make it." Tony took the older man's coat.

"Let's just have a fair game. I came to play. Who's the dealer?" Monty asked.

"Maurice." Tony pointed toward the dealer who nodded in acknowledgement.

"Everybody trust Maurice?" Monty addressed the room of men.

"As long as Maurice deals a good game I have no problems with him." Big Teddy from Alabama said in his loud drawl.

"It's a game of chance." Junior Boy said his youthful face belying his forty four years.

"Well, gentlemen before we begin can I offer you all a drink?" Tony asked.

"Rum and coke for me." Monty said.

"I'll have Scotch neat." Junior Boy replied.

"Milk." said Silent Eddie.

All of the men stopped and laughed.

"Ulcer." Silent Eddie confessed.

Tony shrugged, "Get the man a glass of milk." He nodded to Mona who sat quietly in the corner.

"If you could put a raw egg in it that would be good." Silent Eddie added.

"Jesus!" Tony grimaced.

As Mona headed for the door. "Get me a drink as well, the usual."

Mona nodded and walked downstairs toward the bar.

Tony didn't ask Howard the Jew if he wanted anything to drink. He didn't trust anybody and brought his own drinks. Tony learned a long time ago not to be offended. Howard had been poisoned years back by a prostitute who fleeced him. He had reason to be edgy. He didn't talk much but he usually came with the most cash.

The drinks arrived and Mona took her usual spot in the corner. She had packed up both cars and was prepared to leave but she wanted to stay with Tony and leave together. He agreed thinking that the storm was overblown news and that they would probably have to only stay away for one night. This would be the last game of the season and the money would be laundered there at the club. It was time to do business.

"You ready man?" Kevin put his cap on and checked his guns. They stood in the alleyway next to the secret entrance to the game.

"I'm as ready as I'm going to be". Bertrand said sweating profusely under the hot knit cap.

"Walk quietly." Kevin admonished him as he jimmied the lock easily. There was no one there in the entrance which was a surprise. Monty usually bought his goons with him but the hurricane had made him careless. They crept up the narrow stairway. It was so quiet that both men turned and looked at each other. Had the location been changed? Kevin gestured that they should keep moving forward. They heard a movement, a ceiling fan?

"Now!" Kevin shouted.

He kicked in the door and Bertrand rushed in after him holding two Colt 45's.

"Ya'll put your hands up and no one will get hurt!" He screamed almost hysterically.Silent Eddie and Junior Boy threw down their cards.

"What the hell is this?" Monty asked Tony.

"Put your hands up motherfucker!" Kevin yelled pointing the gun at Monty's head.

Monty slowly raised his hands up. Howard the Jew reached behind his back for his gun.

"Try it and I'll blow your fucking head off man! Drop on the floor!" Kevin kicked the chair from beneath Howard and held the gun to his head.

Tony put his hands up almost casually. He was studying the bigger man. There was something familiar about him. There were five briefcases in the corner. Kevin backed slowly toward them. He kicked one down and knelt down to open it. As he opened it he saw that there was stacks of hundred dollar bills. "Jackpot!" He breathed. He closed it and kicked it over to Bertrand. He picked up two cases and handed another to Bertrand. He took the remaining three cases.

"If anyone follows us out of here we'll blow you're heads off. We have two men posted outside." Kevin smiled beneath his cap.

"I won't have to follow you Bertrand, I know where you work. I'll just come by and pay a visit." Tony said coldly.

Both men were stunned that he had been recognized. Kevin turned around aimed his gun and pulled the trigger. Tony fell to the ground on his knees. Mona screamed. In the heat of the moment Howard the Jew reached his gun and fired two rounds into Kevin's head. The blood exploded over everything.

Bertrand turned and ran down the narrow stairway. He ran to the back alley into the pouring rain. He ran for his life, he knew that Kevin was dead. As he started the engine his only thought was getting out of the city.

"Down home where a nigger could get lost." He pointed his car toward Plaquemines Parish. He didn't have time to think. He didn't have time to fear the hurricane. He only had time to look at the briefcase and drive.

Tony lay on the floor bleeding from his chest and shoulder. Mona leaned over him crying.

"Stupid nigger, didn't he think I'd recognize him?" Tony asked. Sirens were approaching the club. Someone had called the police or ambulance or both.

"You set this whole thing up didn't you Mona?" Tony asked.

"No Tony, don't say that." Mona cried.

"I'm going to live Mona, and then I'm going to kill you." Tony's blue eyes looked deeply into Mona's.

"Like you killed my husband?" Mona asked.

Chapter Thirteen

"I've been feeling like this for a long time Sugar." Remy encircled her waist. She could feel the warmth of his touch. "I want you to be a part of my life." Remy kissed her gently as he pulled her closer. Sugar Doll felt her body pulsating with desire. She knew that she wanted him too. "I know that you have been well protected and..." his voice trailed off. Sugar Doll placed her finger on his mouth.

"I feel the same way." She said. Remy grasped her in an urgent kiss his desire flowing through him. He kissed her neck as he trailed down to the swell of her breast. Sugar Doll gave a gasp in anticipation, she wanted him to go farther. He stopped and looked up at her.

"I know you haven't been with anyone else and I want to make you mine." His face flushed with desire as his blues eyes gazed intently into hers. She caressed his forehead.

"I want to be yours." Sugar Doll breathed in as the rain poured down furiously.

Remy kissed her gently his tongue seeking the warmth of her mouth. He kissed her for a long and tender moment. He unbuttoned the front of her blouse. She gasped as he kissed her between each button. The butterfly kisses created a heat in her as Remy kissed her skin so lightly. Her heart raced as he came to the final button.

"I love you cher," Remy whispered into her ear.

"What in the hell am I doing?" Bertrand could hardly see as he drove down the narrow river road. The rain was blinding. The windshield wipers were like two tiny sticks moving back and forth slowly. He was tempted to turn them off as the rain pelted heavily; it looked as though someone were on the roof of the car with a huge bucket of water. He was reminded of a car wash. He crept along the highway fearful that someone may still be down in the parish and that he was on the wrong side of the road. The ditches were filling with water and overflowing onto the old highway. Fear tingled down Bertrand's spine. He drove toward the old high school that had withstood so many hurricanes in the past. As he turned down the familiar highway he saw that there was a huge gate surrounding the school. He hadn't recalled this gate before today. He got out of the car and walked toward the gate to see the huge pad lock there. He looked at the high fence thinking to jump it. "Who you kidding fat boy?" He said disgusted with himself. He was soaked but it felt good from the heat of the car and his own fear. The rain dripped sense into his brain. He thought of the story of old Uncle Charlie riding out the storm on a tugboat. He thought that this seemed even better than hiding out in the old school which was probably full of snakes and raccoons and all kinds of spiders. He shuddered at the thought. He got back into the car with a renewed sense of direction. The sky was an angry purple and the rain was unrelenting. The cool feeling he'd gotten when he was out of the car now turned into damp discomfort. He remembered Mr. White had a tugboat near the dock. He didn't think that Mr. White would mind so he headed for the Venice dock to prepare for the storm. With any luck there would be food on the boat as they were usually stocked for the crew. "Man this is going to be easy!" the image of Kevin's handsome dark face flashed into his mind. Kevin was dead, and he was wanted. The feeling of salvation dissipated as he drove slowly down the narrow river road leaving the school behind him. His first instinct had been right. Had he stayed at the school he would have run into the Young's a Vietnamese family who had cut through the south side of the fence. Bertrand had only been a few yards away from the cut.

Tony was transported to Charity Hospital as the old folks called it. It was now Central something or other. Sometimes after hundreds of years as an establishment it's best to just leave good enough alone. It's like Muhammad Ali, the old folks still knew him as Cassius Clay and that was that. Mona sat silently by Tony thinking about all that had happened. She couldn't believe that kind, fat and bungling Bertrand would be involved in something like this. She'd known him as a boy and sometimes he even came to her club. He was always respectful and gave her information on Sugar Doll. She couldn't stand to see this happen. She wouldn't stand to see it happen. Tony hadn't breathed a word to anyone about who had done this thing. The other goons had scattered even before the police had come. The storm outside was worse than ever. Tony had severe trauma but was put into the hallway. He was sweating profusely. It was hot but it was a remarkable thing for a man whose motto was "Never let them see you sweat." People passed him as though a gunshot wound was nothing remarkable. She sat next to the bed. She'd seen the look in Tony's eyes when she'd accused him of Karl's murder so many years ago. It rang true and his eyes confirmed it. He didn't say anything else before he went unconscious. Something inside of her had always known. The generosity, the filtering of conversation about Karl. The change in behavior toward Sugar Doll. She'd known all along but then she didn't want to know. She didn't want to realize that her "savior" was also her condemner. The man who stole the spirit of a kind and funny young man. She didn't want to believe it but now painfully she did. "Why had he stuck with her all of those years? Guilt? Love?" She felt disgust for the man she'd loved for so long and now another relative was in trouble.

The lights went out. Everyone in the hospital broke into a frenzy with nurses running all over the place. She heard the word transported several times. Nurses began carting out patients. "Tony needs surgery! I should do something." She looked frantically around but no one seemed to notice her. She should reach out, but then she saw Bertrand's round innocent face and she sat back down quietly, invisibly. She reached for her purse and she walked away not looking back.

"You live by the sword, you die by the sword" Mona said this under her breath even as she knew Tony would die right there on that blood soaked bed.

Big Ma rang Bertrand for what seemed like the hundredth time. "Where is that boy?" She was becoming agitated. The storm had driven them to a hotel but she was able to afford her own room. It was good because she loved her privacy. It was bad because she knew that all of this worry with no one to talk to would bring up her pressure. Her head began to hurt which she knew was already a sign of problems. She reached into her little plastic sandwich bag which carried the bulk of her medications. She took the pressure pills and took off her glasses. "Nothing I can do Lawd." But she knew that something was terribly wrong. Why hadn't Sugar Doll tried to call her? She was the only reason she had the damned phone in the first place. She knelt beside her bed to pray. "Lawd Jesus, my children are out there in the storm and your word says that you will never forsake us or leave us as orphans in the storm. Bring them to safety Jesus, precious Lord. I beg for you to take them out of the eye of the storm." Big Ma remained on side of the bed and as a sign of faith she did not cry. She got up and went to look out of the window expectantly.

Bertrand wiped the sweat from his brow. He drove down the path to old Fort Jackson. As he drove up the graveled highway he realized that he was not in the best place. The rain was coming down in buckets and the wind had picked up considerably. He shook off his feeling of dread. If Uncle Charlie could ride out a storm so could he. He climbed the small hill that was the levee. As he curved the corner of the levee he saw just how much the river had risen. He was afraid. Then he saw the tugboat in the distance and increased his pace in the old car. The big gray rocks spit out from under the tires. He imagined himself in the warmth of the tugboat and the rocking of the water and he felt hopeful. "Everything will be all right once I set foot on the boat." The Venice dock all of a sudden looked like home.

Sugar Doll woke up with a start. A cold sense of dread ran over her as she turned to feel the warmth of Remy's body sleeping peacefully next to her. The feeling passed and she was filled with love. She leaned over to kiss him gently on the neck. He stirred, "Look here cher, if you gonna be starting up with me again we can ride the storm out right here in the French Quarters." Remy pulled her over his shoulder and playfully kissed her. Thunder cracked loudly outside.

"We should leave Remy, it's not safe". Sugar Doll looked worriedly out of the window at the obvious brewing storm.

"Relax hon, God ain't gonna let nothing happen to the French Quarters." Remy purred unconcerned.

"You promised my momma that you would get me out of town." Sugar Doll sat upright determined not to be lured into the sexy warmth of Remy's arms.

"When you are right, you are right. A promise is a promise, c'mon, get your things together and we can go. I'm not taking nothing cause I know it will pass over us but I understand how you feel baby and I always want you to feel safe with me." Remy stood up and gave Sugar Doll a chaste peck on the forehead. "Oh, and I love you Sugar Doll." Remy winked at her his beautiful eyes sparkling.

The phone rang breaking the quiet of the moment. The rain outside was a symphony of water spattering and wind. Remy pointed at Sugar Doll's purse. "It's yours honey. Probably your momma. Tell her we are on our way." Remy said worried for the first time. Miss Mona was no one to play with and he realized his error in judgment.

"Oh, now you're scared? A mean ole hurricane does nothing to you but now you are scared of Hurricane Mona. That's funny." Sugar Doll reached for her purse and pulled out her cell phone. "Hello," she purred enjoying the moment.

"Hello?" "Where the hell are you gal?" It was Big Ma's voice shouting angrily through the phone. Sugar Doll knew that the anger was more worry but it didn't stop her from sitting upright.

"I've been worried sick and your cousin Bertrand is nowhere to be found." Big Ma shouted even though relief flooded her being.

"I'm in the French Quarters Big Ma." Sugar Doll interrupted.

"The French Quarters? You need to get out of New Orleans. Haven't you been watching the news? I'm surprised I got you. All of the circuits have been busy. The Lawd has answered my prayer that's all! We are in Alexandria. You need to get out of there!" Big Ma screamed furious that the child was still in harms way.

"We are leaving right now. We are going to Gonzales." Sugar Doll tried to soothe her grandmother. Remy made a come here sign and they both headed for the door as she talked to her grandmother on the phone.

"You and Mona?" Big Ma asked.

"No, me and Remy." Sugar Doll said cringing.

"Put him on the phone right now." Big Ma demanded.

Sugar Doll reluctantly handed the phone to Remy mouthing "Big Ma." He nodded understanding and took the phone.

"Hello there Big Ma!" Remy intoned cheerfully.

"Now you looka here Mister Remy Gaudeaux, that's my grandbaby you got there. You need to get out of town right now. I may not be able to reach ya'll again but I'm telling you to get her out of there now." Big Ma demanded.

"We are on our way out of here right now ma'am. You have my word that I'll take right good care of her." Remy said sincerely.

"Well, I do hope so, cause I don't want to know what she is doing with you and not her momma." Big Ma expressed the concern that had already crossed her mind when Sugar Doll told her who she was with. She knew that it was inevitable. She could see the way they looked at each other on that day they came to visit. "Now put Sugar Doll back on the phone."

"Yes, ma'am." Remy handed the phone to Sugar Doll.

"Since you are closer maybe you can try to reach your cousin Bertrand to see what is the matter. It's not like him to not call or to get word to me. He was in Baton Rouge but he's not answering the phone. I feel like something bad has happened to him." Big Ma said.

"Oh, he's all right. You know Bertrand is afraid of bad weather, particularly lightening. He's probably hiding somewhere, but I'll try to call him and when we get to Gonzales I'll try to call you again, so keep your line open." Sugar Doll advised.

"Who else I'm gonna talk to anyway? I just got this phone for your benefit." Big Ma smiled for the first time, her sweet little girl was safe.

"Alright, I'll call you in a couple of hours. When the storm passes we will drive up there to come and get you." Sugar Doll promised.

"Be careful. I love you Sugar Doll." Big Ma hung up the phone praising the Lord for letting her hear her baby's voice.

The air inside the tugboat was musty. The smell of crude oil was heavy and insistent curling its thick smell up Bertrand's nostrils and making him feel nauseous. There were ropes strewn everywhere, all over the floor. The boat was a mess. A tool box lay half opened. The place looked like someone had left in a hurry. True to form the key to the cabin was under the mat. Southerners were such trusting folks. Bertrand had never thought once about possibly being locked out of the boat. He didn't have the criminal bent to break a window. "Yet you can break into a card game full of gangsters and pull a gun." He said this aloud punishing himself for following Kevin's desperate plan. So he would have lost the bar, now look at him stuck in a storm. He was a big man but he shivered, not from cold but from fear.

Marsalas arrived at the hospital one hour after Mona had left. His men spread out to search for Tony in the confusion. He would take him to his private physician if necessary. He felt his anger rise as he thought of that bitch.

"Boss, we found him in a room. It's pretty bad." Frank grabbed his arm and led him in the direction of the room.

As Marsalas approached the room he smelled death. He knew that there was no hope. Tony tried to lift his head but his breathing was ragged and raspy. Marsalas approached the bed slowly. His heart beat harder. Tony had been like a son to him.

"Marsalas I did not tell Mona about the operation. I swear on my mother's grave."

"You'll swear on just about everything right now. That's a serious wound you've got there. Do you think it's wise to protect her now?" Marsalas shook his head.

Tony felt his resolve weaken. He felt the blood seeping into the bed from his side. The bandage was doing nothing. His mind raced. What if she did know? What if she planned the whole thing? It didn't seem like her. He'd said things in anger but in reality, he trusted her. He didn't want to hurt her. Marsalas studied him for a long moment.

"I told you to never think of a woman as stupid. For years I thought that you were skimming off of the top but I forgave that, honor among thieves. It's your nature. I was proud of you." Marsalas hesitated and looked carefully at Tony. "Maybe you ain't as smart as I give you credit for – maybe she was doing the stealing?" Marsalas leaned on the bed.

"No, Marsalas, it was me all the way. If it was her I would tell you." Tony rasped. Marsalas wasn't buying it.

Tony passed out sweat dripping from his forehead. One of Marsalas' men grabbed a passing nurse.

"Everyone is vacating the hospital sir. The hurricane is going to hit the city." The nurse came into the room and took Tony's vitals.

"He's very weak and won't be able to be moved. He needs a doctor." The nurse said.

"Then get one!" Marsalas ordered. The big goon manhandled the nurse into the hallway. Marsalas watched as Tony's breath caught and stopped. He put his fingers on his pulse. It was very weak. Marsalas shook his head and nodded to his goon. He walked from the room and into the steady rain. He had one thought, "Kill Mona."

The rain poured down in a steady stream. Sugar Doll felt free and independent. She had a boyfriend! She looked over the hood of the car at Remy who looked just as free as she felt. Her body still zinged with his touch. She was happy that she had asked him to wait before they became intimate. She was disappointed that he looked relieved. He winked at her rain trickling down his face. The sound of sirens did not cause any alarm because the sheriff's office was probably still evacuating residents. It was early evening even the color of the sky was a deep angry purple.

"Do you think that Mona and Tony are still at the club?" Remy asked.

"Probably, I know that Mona mentioned a big card game, so I doubt they are leaving until right before the storm hits. They are packed and ready to go. No one thinks that this hurricane is at bad as it sounds." Sugar Doll said as she got into the dry car. The air freshener smelled of orange.

"Mayor Thompson begs to differ honey. He's been all over the news telling people to get the hell out of Dodge." Remy cracked.

"Maybe he's right, but look at the streets, it looks like a lot of people have decided to ride the storm out right here in the Quarters or at home." Sugar Doll looked at the street noting all of the people who were running around.

"These are people who can't afford to go honey. They would if they could." The couple drove down the narrow street toward Mona's restaurant. They noticed police tape and a group of onlookers.

"What the hell is going on?" Remy exclaimed when he saw the crowd.

"Maybe they got robbed." Sugar Doll said prophetically.

"People are too busy running from the hurricane to rob anybody." Remy said.

They got out of the car to go to see what the problem was at the restaurant.

"They shot the owner." A bystander said.

"What?" Sugar Doll cried.

"The owner was shot in the stomach, that's what they are saying." The bystander disappeared in the crowd to go to his home to start packing up. "People always got time for violence" he said to himself as he walked down the street toward his own flat in the quarter. He was prepared to go but curiosity had gotten the best of him.

"Oh Remy!" Sugar Doll screamed.

"Now hold on a minute, we are going to go and find her. The closest hospital is Charity so I know they took her there. Let's go!" Remy opened the car door for Sugar Doll. He looked at the club all dark inside and felt the feeling of shock ebb away from his body. Tony was a gangster after all and this was something to be expected but poor Mona.

They raced across town to the hospital. The entrance was blocked so they had to find a parking spot on the street. They ran holding hands to the hospital only to experience complete chaos. Nurses and people were running to and fro. People were being taken out of the hospital.

"Excuse me where can I find a gunshot victim?" Sugar Doll asked upset and shaken. She cried as the nurse just walked past her ignoring her completely. An old woman in wheelchair reached out and touched her hand. The touch was familiar and kind.

"Honey just look in the hallways. I'm sad to say that the people here don't care for us poor folks. They ain't taking no patients in right now no way." The old lady's eyes were gray and watery.

"Thank you, thank you for answering me." Sugar Doll gently touched her hand.

"Let's break up and search the hallways and rooms." Remy suggested. Sugar Doll nodded and took off in the opposite direction. She walked up one hall and then the next. There were many old people in corners. It looked as though someone just put them there for safe keeping. Remy saw a blood soaked sheet. He walked toward it slowly. The body that lay beneath had already been covered by some good Samaritan. As Remy pulled back the bloody sheet he saw Tony's pale face. The face was so unlike the lively one he had just had drinks with just hours before that he stepped back in shock. Tony grabbed Remy's wrist sending shockwaves through Remy's entire being. Whoever had pulled that sheet over Tony had been premature.

"Bertrand did this to me. It was Bertrand." Tony whispered as loudly as he could even as his life poured out of him. In rasping gasps Tony spoke his last words. "Bertrand." Remy tried to pull out of the grasp not wanting to believe the words that were spoken but knowing deep inside they were true. The reality of Tony's impending death made it true. He turned away from that truth. As he did so he saw Sugar Doll slowly approaching, warily wondering if he held her mother. He looked back down at Tony's face and there was the glassy sightless eyes that spoke only of death.

Chapter Fourteen

The winds picked up and the boat rollicked back and forth. Bertrand felt himself become nauseous for the fourth time. He was deeply regretting those hamburgers he had earlier. He had forgotten about his seasickness. He had forgotten that he wasn't a strong swimmer. He thought of good old Uncle Charlie fighting the good fight. He was a seasoned seaman. "You are the dumbest niggah I ever did know." Bertrand imitated Uncle Charlie's high pitched cackling voice. He thought that this once Uncle Charlie had been right. "I wonder if Tony is all right." He wondered aloud for the first time. There would be hell to pay if a Marsalas was murdered. He was in enough trouble as it was but when things cooled down he planned to go back to the city and pretend that nothing had happened. He looked at his surroundings and realized that it would be a long hurricane. The wind gust outside was picking up. He needed some fresh air to help quell the nausea he was feeling. He tried to balance his heavy body as he walked to the cabin door. He looked outside of the window; the water had come up on the bow of the boat. He could see that the water level was extremely high and at a dangerous level. He would have to untie from the pier in order to ride the storm out in the first place. He ran outside to the pier and tried to loosen the thick rope but it was as tight as nails. Fear sprang into his heart not for the first time this morning. He went back into the cabin and found an axe. He went back to the rope and began hacking away at it. It began to give. "You stupid old rope, c'mon now." Bertrand shouted losing his temper. He was afraid. The waves crashed against the boat. The storm had picked up considerably since the hour he had arrived to the dock. The boat was rocking against the rope as though it were a horse trying to get away from its owner.

Bertrand continued hacking away when in success the rope gave. He hopped on the pier to give the boat a push. This really wasn't necessary because the current was so strong that the boat had already begun to move toward the sea. Bertrand glanced back at his car. He thought for a moment that he should just give up and drive back to the city or Baton Rouge or Tennessee. He turned and jumped on the boat. His fate was set and he would have to ride it out to the end.

"Oh my God Remy, what happened? Did he tell you?" Sugar Doll felt herself grow weak at the sight of Tony's dead body. Remy closed Tony's eyes and then pulled the cover over his face.

"I don't know Sugar Doll. He said that Bertrand did it. Bertrand." Remy repeated unbelieving.

"What? That 's ridiculous, Bertrand doesn't have a violent bone in his body and why would he kill Tony?" Sugar Doll asked outraged.

"I don't know Sugar Doll. I don't think Bertrand would do such a thing. He was in a lot of debt though. Maybe something happened. There is only one way to find out and that's to find Mona." Remy deduced.

"I've looked everywhere and she doesn't seem to be here. They are transporting people to another hospital. The hurricane is getting closer and it's dangerous. Oh Remy, I'm scared." Sugar Doll cried and fell into his arms.

Mona walked up Canal Street searching for a taxi but it was a fruitless search. Her bar wasn't too far away but the stinging rain made her uncomfortable. She still had on her high heels. Too many things were going on for her to change into more comfortable attire. "I wonder if that bastard is dead." Mona thought to herself. She let out an unexpected wail. She cried bitterly as she realized that she had loved that man. She couldn't see but this time it wasn't because of the rain, it was her grief and her tears that clouded her vision. She stumbled into the French Quarter crying against a gray stoned building. She fell to the ground crying uncontrollably. For the first time in her life she was utterly alone. She thought of Tony's blue flashing eyes and his charming smile and she cried even harder. She realized that what she had felt for him all of those years was pride. Pride that he had chosen her. He was addicted to her as she was to him. No matter what fights they had they always came together in passion and love. There were many women who loved Tony but only one who he loved and that had been Mona. He had set her up with her own business and then frequented the place so much because he loved being around her. Her energy was wonderful. He had loved her beauty but it was her intelligence that kept him coming back to his caramel colored lady. The guys laughed at him for his guma but he never had a wife to cheat on and he rarely cheated on Mona. When she found out about any affair he would drop the woman and deny her completely. Theirs had been a love story. Even the way Mona walked out on him in his final moments was what Tony considered class. A clingy, sad woman made him sweat but Mona with her steely reserve had left him just the way that he liked it, independent and alone. Now here she fell on a street corner crying for the man she realized she had always loved. She didn't weaken and turn to the hospital. She straightened herself and wiped her eyes as she stood in the pouring rain and she ran toward home, toward safety.

"Katrina has been upgraded to a Category 4 Hurricane." The news report droned on and both Elise and Patrice hugged each other. The Superdome was so hot that it felt like a sauna. Patrice and Elise found themselves wishing they had gone with Sugar Doll. Rain had begun to leak through the ceiling and the sense of fear was palpable. The wind gusts outside had picked up considerably and both girls held onto each other although some of that wind would be welcomed in this dank hole. They moved from their high spots because the water was dripping down on them.

"Is that woman dead?" Elise asked pointing to an elderly woman who seemed to be propped up clumsily to the chair.

"Quit it! She ain't dead, she's just sleeping stupid." Patrice responded annoyed.

"Then that's a deep sleep honey." Elise answered cynically.

The girls both openly stared at the old woman. Bobby Joe and Tommy both approached the girls interested in this new sport, "What are ya'll staring at?"

"That lady over there looks...well she looks... Patrice stammered feeling faint.

"She looks dead." Bobby Joe finished her sentence.

"Let's move ya'll. We found a spot that isn't wet and smells a hellava lot better. We been looking for ya'll for a minute." Bobby Joe said taking Patrice's hand.

"For True?" Elise reached for Tommy's hand who promptly avoided her touch.

"Yeah, like it's dangerous here man. All of the homeboys from the 9th ward and Algiers are here and we thought about ya'll all alone and stuff. We gonna protect you." Bobby Joe said winking back at Elise.

"Why thank you." Elise said stepping forward between Patrice and Bobby Joe. "It's a scary place and we were starting to be afraid." She took Bobby Joe's hand, who was much too polite to take it away. He glanced over at Patrice. The four of them walked down the long stairway of the stadium to the east side of the dome. Tommy turned on his radio.

"We've got to find Mona." Remy said as he took Sugar Doll's hand. "The only place besides the French Quarters she could go would be the Superdome."

Sugar Doll wasn't as certain as Remy. They were in their car but the wind and the rain was overwhelming. Signs were straining at their bases and the traffic lights whipped back and forth at an alarming rate. "The French Quarters are already experiencing wind damage and fallen trees. Please be advised that the Quarters are closed to the public." A news reporter droned on as Remy hit his hand on the steering wheel. Sugar Doll changed the station. "Mayor Thompson has ordered a mandatory evacuation. The hurricane has been upgraded as a category five and is expected to create a state of emergency."

"Oh Remy, what are we going to do?" Sugar Doll cried thinking about the fact that the club was on the tree lined Royal Street.

"We are going to go to the Quarters to see if Mona is still there and then we are going to head to Gonzales before it's too late." Remy nosed his car toward the Quarters. The rain fell down heavily but it wasn't as bad there as had been reported. It was no more than a bad thunderstorm. As they came close to the club there was a tree strewn in front of the narrow street so Remy just stopped the car where they were and hopped out quickly. He looked back in and signaled for Sugar Doll to stay where she was. He walked around the perimeter of the building and could see that it was locked up tightly. He went to the back alley and saw Mona's Lincoln Continental packed up to the roof. He walked to the back stairway and yelled up, "Mona! Mona!" There was no answer. He knocked on the door and the adjacent window and saw no signs of life. He knocked harder and stood and waited. He shrugged and walked back down the steps to the front street. Sugar Doll was standing in the rain holding her arms. She looked beautiful. "Honey, get back in the car, she isn't there." Remy ran up to her and led her back to her side of the car.

The storm was getting worse and it was important to find shelter. Remy and Sugar Doll drove up to Claiborne street to hit the expressway but were met with a blockade. There were orange signs all over but no one to give direction. Remy realized that he had waited too long and that they had to find immediate shelter. He knew that the French Quarters were on higher ground and so returned to his apartment on Vieux Carre at Dumaine and Royal. Sugar Doll sat silently. "Honey, it looks like we are going to have to ride this thing out here. After the storm we will go to the Superdome to look for your mama I promise."

"I'm scared Remy, are you sure we'll be alright here?" She shuddered, thinking about the possibility of drowning.

"Honey, the French Quarters have survived yellow fever and numerous hurricanes and it's still standing. We are on higher ground and couldn't be in a better place. I'm going to board up the windows to protect us from flying debris but we'll be okay." Remy took her hand as he led her back up to his second floor apartment. The memory of their last evening together came rushing back to him but he suppressed it. There was no more time for playing.

The Young family sat shivering in the corner of the old high school. They were afraid and somehow silence helped that fear. Mai Young looked over at her husband with disgust. She felt like a refugee all over again. Why hadn't he saved some of the money they made in the store? She knew that it was useless to ask herself this. Ever since that damned Casino had opened in the city he couldn't miss a night and thinking himself a rich man he always bet high. He had always been so responsible. She looked at her children sitting there afraid and alone. She wanted to reach out to them but she didn't want to scare them by doing something out of character. The wind outside raged. The rain and the lightening had gotten even worse. They should have at least gone to a storm shelter or the Superdome. Mr. Young was afraid of the area. He had been mugged by young, muscular black kids and he never wanted to go close to it again. So the decision had been made to go to the old school. They at least had enough food for a month and water. This was the benefit of owning a store. They sat next to the small fire her husband Huy had built for them. She was too angry to meet his eyes.

The boat frolicked over the water like a playful pony. Bertrand no longer had anything else to vomit and so was reduced to painful dry heaves. "Lawd have mercy, how long is this going to go on?" He had drifted somewhere in the middle of the river. The tugboat seemed sturdy and big but that didn't stop waves from crashing onto the deck. What was he thinking about coming on the water in the eye of the hurricane. He turned on his transistor radio and heard the dreadful news that it would be a category five hurricane but now it was too late to turn around and woefully he realized that he knew little about handling a boat. He realized that playing on your father's boat every summer didn't qualify one to handle a tugboat. The first big wave that came toward the boat looked like a small wall. Bertrand try to steer clear of it but it came straight across and appeared to have no end. He was surprised to see that the tugboat plowed through the wave and kept going. He made the sign of the cross "God, I'm a man, I've sinned and I ask for your forgiveness." Bertrand put his head down in reverence. When he looked up a 30 foot wall of water crashed down on him slamming the boat into mere splinters.

Mona walked toward her house on Dauphine Street in the Maringy neighborhood. It was down river east of the Quarter. She rarely used the house because she preferred to stay in her apartments in the bar. She couldn't bear to return to the scene of her lover's shooting. The wind forced her to walk sideways but now she could see her house in the distance. She saw boarding on the windows and was grateful to her kind neighbor an elderly white gentleman who kept a look-out on her place. She paid him a little each month and that supplemented his pension check. He'd offered to do it for free but she felt better being able to give something to the man she had known since she was a young woman.

Finally getting to the door she leaned against it in exhaustion. The wind had to be about 50 mph. She didn't know how she'd walked through it once she stood on her porch. She leaned heavily against the door still feeling the grief of losing Tony. She heard a tapping and looked over to see Mr. Reniar looking out at her in concern. She motioned for him to come over to her. The old man closed the blinds and disappeared for a moment. He reappeared with a large umbrella and wearing a big coat. It wasn't cold at all but she supposed his age caused him to have to wear it. "I thought you had gotten out of town honey." He squinted up at her through his enormous glasses.

"No, there was some trouble at the club sir. I've decided to sit it out here. Do you want to join me? I have a pantry full of food and a freezer full of beer." Mona said hopefully, she didn't want to be alone.

"Do you have coffee?" The old man asked.

"Yes sir, I sure do." Mona nodded relieved.

"Well then I could use the company as well." The old man took out his spare key for Mona's house and opened the door.

"I'll be right back honey, put on some coffee. I have to go and get my medicine and my wife's picture." The old man winked and walked out again before Mona could stop him.

She walked into the house she'd bought with her successful business. Tony rarely came to this house. It was her sanctuary. As she walked into the living room the plush sofa looked so inviting that she didn't bother to change into dry clothes. She stretched out on the couch and fell into a deep sleep.

Big Ma had fallen asleep on the double bed fully dressed. She had gone to bed praying for her children. She was dreaming. She saw herself as a young girl of about fourteen. She was on the levee playing and she knew that her mother didn't want her there but she remained playing and throwing rocks onto the water. She saw a funnel cloud coming up the channel of the river but could not run. Her legs were rooted to the spot. The tornado on the water drew closer to her splitting the water like Moses on the Red Sea. The tornado came off of the water and hit the land splitting the trees and heading for her. She began to run her heart pounding. She turned back to look and thought of Lot's wife. She did not turn into a pillar of salt but the tornado was right there and it pulled her up into its belly. She whirled around and around and around. She screamed. Big Ma sat up in the bed her face pouring sweat. "Bertrand!"

The night proved long. The wind whipped through the French Quarters snapping trees and pulling up signs from the ground. Wires popped from their place and the world was at war with nature. Inside the Superdome Patrice and Elise hugged each other as the windowless dome made them feel as though they had been caught in a tunnel. Bobby Joe and Tommy sat quietly looking up at the ceiling which was dripping water. Elise imagined the storm as gigantic monster, the howling of the wind and the occasional loud thuds which hit the building sent her into a panic. She cried silently as Patrice calmly held her hand.

"We gotta get outta here!" Elise screamed becoming hysterical. "We are going to drown here!" Elise stood her heavy body dragging Patrice with her. Patrice tried to calm her but Elise was out of control. Bobby Joe stood blocking her way. He was no more than sixteen years but massively built he grabbed Elise and shook her.

"Calm down girl, we's all right. We is going to get outta this. After the storm pass ya'll coming with us. Calm the hell down!" Bobby Joe held her tightly. Elise dissolved into a crying fit. The drone of the radio continued to report on what they heard outside.

"Forecasters fear that the levees won't hold Katrina. The Army Core of Engineers had been warned about the state of the levees. The Crescent City could very well end up under water." The newscaster droned on inflicting many with new found fears. People in the Superdome were huddled in their family groups. Some people prayed together holding hands while others talked trying to drown out the sound of the raging storm outside.

"As soon as the storm passes we are going to get out of here." Bobby Joe repeated looking into Elise's eyes.

"Remy are you done yet?" Sugar Doll sat on the plush carpet of his apartment as he stood at the final set of windows nailing boards to them from the inside.

"Almost Sugar, fix me a drink will you?" Remy asked thirsty for more than just water.

"I'm scared." Sugar Doll said for what seemed like the hundredth time.

"I know you are honey, but trust me, we will be okay. Nothing's happened yet has it?" Remy asked.

"It sounds bad out there and now I'm worried. I have a terrible feeling."Sugar Doll admitted to the ominous feeling she had had all morning.

"Well, let me see, we are stuck here, you saw your stepfather die and we don't know where your momma is. Of course you are feeling upset honey. It's only natural but I'm here for you and I'm not going anywhere." Remy said this to be a comfort but he really just reminded Sugar Doll of all that had happened. Her face darkened.

He hammered the last nail into the plywood and put down his hammer. He walked over to Sugar Doll and hugged her.

"I'm sorry baby; your momma is probably halfway to Baton Rouge by now. She probably took Tony's car in all of the excitement and forgot her own. Don't worry at all. It's time we get some sleep. It's almost morning and neither of us has slept. The storm's coming whether we like it or not." Remy lifted Sugar Doll by the elbow and led her to the bedroom. He took off his shirt but left on his slacks. As they crawled into bed he hugged her tightly from behind and they nodded off to the rhythm of the rain and the wind.

The Young family huddled around a makeshift fire their father had made for them. Mai Young still averted the eyes of her husband who was now staring at her intently. He knew that she considered him a failure and that this final insult would probably end their twenty-five year marriage. He remembered the first day he had come to America. He remembered working like a dog and being called a yellow nigger. He remembered Mai's face on their wedding day. He would have wept but he didn't want Mai to see his pain. The wind outside was fierce and the water was rising. They had already climbed to the second floor of the old school. A loud boom cracked the air with electricity and then as he looked up he saw the building collapsing. A gush of water flattened the roof and the Young family died where they sat in a circle.

Chapter Fifteen

There was a crackling sound. Sugar Doll listened intently. The wind was still howling but now there was something more. Remy lay asleep next to her. She got up gently in search of the sound. As she walked into the living room she felt a shiver even though it was quite warm. She saw the little radio on the counter where Remy had left it. She tried to adjust the dial to a coherent station but still just the crackling noise emitted from it. She put it down and wondered if there was still electricity. She went to the refrigerator. It was still cold but the power was off.

"Katrina made landfall at approximately 7 a.m. this morning." The radio began to transmit the information. Sugar Doll turned toward it like she would a welcome friend. They had survived the hurricane. "A levee was breached. We are still investigating but widespread flooding is expected. Wait a minute this just in; a large section of the vital 17th Street Canal levee where it connects to the brand new "hurricane proof" Old Hammond Highway Bridge gave way late Monday morning in Bucktown after Katrina's fiercest winds were well north of it." Sugar Doll ran back to the bedroom where Remy still lay sleeping.

"Remy! Remy!" Sugar Doll pushed him. "Wake up!" Sugar Doll noticed the curl of a smile that always sent her heart aflutter.

"What dahling?" Remy drawled as he pulled her toward him. He was rethinking not making love to her this morning.

"The hurricane made landfall this morning." Sugar Doll said flushed.

"What time is it now?" Remy asked.

"I don't know, the power's out. You left your transistor radio on though. Remy reached for his watch on the side of the bed. It was two o'clock in the afternoon. He sat bolt upright all thoughts of making love leaving him.

"I've got to go outside to see how things turned out." He got up grabbing his shirt on a nearby chair. The windows were still boarded up but the sound of rain was still evident.

"Don't go Remy, it could be dangerous." Sugar Doll begged.

"I won't go far; I just want to look outdoors. Obviously we didn't get too much damage here in the Quarters." He gave her an 'I told you so look.' "I'll be right back Sugar."

He ambled for the door. Sugar Doll stood up, "I'm coming with you." She stated.

"I don't think it's a good idea. Let me do a look see and if it's okay then I'll come back to get you I promise." He kissed her quickly but pushed her away. Sugar Doll accepted his decision but regretted doing that the moment he walked out of the door.

Remy expected to see some debris and tree branches but he didn't expect to see so much glass laying around. The sun was shining through the light rain. "The devil must be beating his wife." Remy repeated the old saying. He stepped out onto the curb to look at his apartment building. Some of the moldings had fallen and the sheetrock portion of the building was chipped but it was still standing. Remy looked up to his apartment windows and saw that most of the glass windows had been broken in the high winds. The boards had protected them. He turned around to look up the street and saw some other people already outside cleaning. There was water but very little. The cars on the street were covered with dead leaves. Remy walked down Tchopatulis street looking into different buildings. He heard music at the end of the street. He ran down to the street corner and there was Bernie's open for business.

"C'mon inside and get yourself a beer before they get hot." Bernie called out to Remy. He was tempted but then he thought of Sugar Doll alone and afraid in the apartment. He waved and shouted, "I'm coming back. Let me get my girlfriend!" Remy smiled his charming smile and ran back up to the apartment. He ran back up the short distance he had traveled and up the three flights of stairs with relative ease. When he walked in the door he saw Sugar Doll standing with her back to him. She looked vulnerable. His joi de vive immediately came crashing down and he went to hold her from behind. Her shoulders tensed. "It's all right Sugar. Bernie's is even selling beer right now."

Sugar Doll swung around, "It's not all right. People are stranded, hundreds have died and my hometown is gone Remy, gone!" Sugar Doll cried into his shoulder.

"No baby, you are wrong. I've just been outside. It's a bad storm for sure but it's not that bad." Remy shrugged trying to comfort Sugar Doll.

Just then the voice of Louisiana's governor Kathleen Blanco rang out from the radio, "Several hundred people have been rescued from rooftops and buildings. If you are with family or in a shelter please stay where you are. Keep safe. If you have tap water please boil it before drinking. We are in a state of emergency and it is important that we all keep calm. Hurricane Katrina has been downgraded to a tropical storm but there are many who need our help." Remy walked over to the radio to turn it off.

"Leave it on Remy." Sugar Doll demanded.

"It's lies Sugar." Remy explained.

"No it's not. Bertrand is out there, Mona, my friends. We have to help. We have to do something." Sugar Doll shored up her strength and looked resolved. She walked toward the door."You heard the governor, if you are in a safe place stay where you are. There is no electricity. I have bottled water and food here. There is glass all over the place downstairs and I'm sure it's worse away from the Quarter. We are 5 feet above sea level Sugar. I knew we would be safe but now with everything that's out there it's best to stay put and wait." Remy reasoned.

"Wait? For what? Wait for help when we are young and can help ourselves? I want to go to the Superdome and find Mona. I want to help my friends Patrice and Elise. I want to get out of this small room." Sugar Doll opened the door and ran down the stairs.

❦

Big Ma paced in her hotel room. She knew that something terrible had happened. The rain was coming down in buckets now. The weather system which had devastated her hometown was now finally making its way up to Baton Rouge. She felt an emptiness that only implied a death as far as she was concerned. She didn't feel a fear for Sugar Doll but Bertrand's image left a heaviness in her heart. She called Reverend Han's room."Pastor, I need you to pray for Bertrand. He's in trouble."

"Now sister, we have been praying for everyone and everything. There is no need to worry about the young people. It is the old and infirm I'm worried about now." Reverend Han couldn't help smiling into the phone. Sister Jones was always concerned about her family and a more loving lady one rarely met. He knew that this small comfort wouldn't stop her but it wouldn't stop him from trying to convince her that he knew what he was talking about in the first place. The television kept showing that their Parish was obliterated. He was happy that they had landed in Alexandria instead of staying in that sinful city New Orleans.

"I feel that something is wrong and I don't know what to do about it." Big Ma cried which was unlike her.

"I know how you feel Sister Jones, but we must be strong hearted. Weeping endures for the night but then joy comes in the morning." He smiled at his favorite comfort phrase.

"Thank you Pastor." Big Ma hung up the phone but the feeling of dread and worry simply would not leave her. She got on her knees to pray again.

Sugar Doll didn't really know what she was doing but she headed out to the street and just as Remy said there was broken glass everywhere. Remy was close on her heels and took her arm. Sugar, there are some places that need boats to travel to in the first place. We need to find what we can to help but first we must be prepared ourselves. The Superdome has over 2000 people there and we will have too much difficulty locating just a few people. I'm more than sure that they don't have anything set up yet. We need to take a wait and see attitude. Please Sugar. Please." Remy tried to reason with Sugar Doll but her mind was made up and she just kept walking even though she didn't have a particular direction.

"Okay, if you insist. Let's see where we can get a boat to go over to the areas we need to make it. They walked toward Canal Street. As they neared the street there were palm trees strewn all over the place. There were police officers on every corner sitting in wait for any looters. One such officer intercepted them. "Where ya'll think ya'll going?" He asked.

"We are going to the Superdome." Sugar Doll said as strongly as she could.

"The Superdome? Ya'll survived the hurricane and you want to try to go to the Superdome? Ya'll are crazy. You may not pass. Please return to your residence. Things are going to get worse before they get better and I can guarantee that a pretty girl like yourself won't last long on these streets. Go home ma'am and sir keep an eye on her. There are rampant murders and rapes going on right now as we speak. This is not a time for anyone to be out of doors. Consider this a warning." The officer turned them around physically.

Remy was in agreement so he didn't argue. He grabbed Sugar Doll by the shoulder and led her in the direction of his apartment. She seemed to give in but then turned in a different direction.

"Where are you going Sugar Doll? You heard the officer. This is not the time to go out aimlessly looking around. Let's wait till things settle and then we can search for you momma and your friends. Please Sugar Doll." Remy pleaded with her. She turned reluctantly around but realized that he was right and that she was being bullheaded. They walked slowly back to his apartment. The radio was still playing on his kitchen counter. It was scratchy and sounded as though two stations had crossed each other. Kathleen Blanco's voice droned on about the need for people to keep their sanity and to wait for help to arrive. Day one of Hurricane Katrina was a nightmare.

Mona woke with a start. She heard a gunshot, loud and obtrusive. She sat bolt upright. She was disoriented. As she blinked she realized that she was in her living room on her own couch. She jumped startled when she felt the presence of someone else. Mr. Renair sat in her La-Z-Boy chair dozing, his eyeglasses hanging onto his nose. It all came crashing back to her. Tony was dead. She imagined that she saw the bullet which penetrated his stomach. She held herself tightly. The hurricane. She got up slowly her legs inexplicably wobbly and then she remembered the long walk in the wind and rain from the hospital. Bang! Boom! Another powerful blast struck and this time she knew it was not a dream. She felt the floor shake. It felt like an earthquake but then she knew better. She instinctively went to the window but realized once pulling open the curtains that they were boarded up and she was closed off to the outside world. There was no flooding on this first floor so she felt sure that the hurricane had missed them. She smelled the welcome scent of coffee and walked toward it. As she poured herself a cup she thought about everything that had happened. Boom! Boom! There was the sound again. She couldn't imagine what it could be. This time she headed for the front door to look out but only saw rain and debris strewn outside her yard. She tried for the lights but there was no power. She walked toward the pantry and pulled out an old radio and batteries. "Good Afternoon." Mr. Renair startled her. She jumped almost dropping the batteries. "Sorry, I didn't mean to scare you." He smiled walking into the kitchen to retrieve a cup to pour himself some coffee.

"Well, you did." Mona said grumpily. "Did you feel that boom?" she asked.

"Yes I did. I most surely did." Mr. Renair took a sip from his coffee thoughtfully. "I believe that they are blowing up the levee." He said shaking his head.

"Why would they do that?" Mona asked.

"To relieve pressure and to save the Quarters. They did it back in1927. It was denied, but it happened." Mr. Renair sat down.

"How do you know?" Mona asked.

"My father told me. They sacrificed the poor to save the rich and now the Quarters are all we have that makes us unique. The View Carre will survive, must survive. To my way of thinking the storm must be pretty bad for them to pull a stunt like that again."

Mona turned the radio on now that she had installed the batteries. "Massive flooding as the levees are breached." Poured from the radio. Mona looked at Mr. Renair who just sipped his coffee.

"Elise, I've got to go to the bathroom." Patrice said getting up to walk down to the next level.

"I'll come with you." Elise stood up to accompany her sister.

"Do you have to go?" Patrice asked annoyed.

"No. All right I'll stay here." Elise sat back down with Bobby Joe. The boys were playing cards again.

"I'll be right back." Patrice said as she descended the stairs.

She turned the corner and had to practically walk over people in the hallway. She went into the bathroom. She finally got a stall at the end of the corridor.

"Hey girl, you sure is fine!" Came an unfamiliar voice who pushed open the stall door.

"Get out of here are you crazy?" Patrice yelled.

"How you gonna call me crazy we ain't even been introduced yet." The muscular black man approached Patrice menacingly. He was on her in a flash pushing her hard against the wall. He covered her mouth with his hand. The cold steel bar pressed hard against her back. He was choking her. Patrice could feel herself screaming but couldn't hear it. The man was taking off her pants. Then a painful push came. She had her eyes closed but quickly opened them to see what the force was. Elise had pulled the man down to the ground and was beating him. Patrice fell on him too. They were both screaming. Other women came forward then kicking and screaming and beating the man who struggled to get away. The man tried to run but was held down by Elise's girth. She was hitting and scratching him blindly. Then a hand appeared who moved her on the side. It was Bobby Joe and Tommy stood beside him. They pushed the man out the door and began beating and kicking him. The man finally broke away from the fray.

Patrice struggled to get her pants up. She was trembling. She cried. Elise stood to help her sister. They hugged. "Let's get out of here!" Patrice cried.

Chapter Sixteen

Sugar Doll paced the room. "We've got to help Remy. The government is doing nothing."

Remy knew that she was right. He had been wracking his brains for ideas on helping. He realized that there were many people stuck in the flood waters and that his little canoe could help many people. He opened up the balcony and picked up the boat. "Let's go." He said and he and Sugar Doll walked out together.

The guys at Bernie's bar were having a good time. In the hours since Remy had seen them their faces had become red from the heat and drinking. "Hey Remy boy, come on now and get yo'self a drink!" One of the locals yelled out to him.

"No thanks man, I'm going to try to help some people with this here canoe." The men raised their glass to Remy as he and Sugar Doll walked by them. They headed toward St. Charles Avenue. It wasn't long before they saw the damage of the hurricane. Cars were filled with water. As they walked the water rose from their ankles to their knees to finally their waists. Sugar Doll got into the canoe as Remy pushed it. When the water became too deep he jumped inside of it. They were on St. Charles Avenue. As they floated by houses taking in the devastation they heard a loud cry. "Help Me! Help Me!" An old lady was sitting on her roof.

"We are coming for you honey." Remy stirred the boat closer.

"Ya'll be careful of them water snakes. I've seen a lot of 'em." The old lady advised.

"She's not exactly inspiring confidence is she? Remy winked at Sugar Doll who laughed. They tied a rope to the boat and Remy climbed up the siding of the house. He thanked God for the wrought iron design of the house which was more like a ladder.

"C'mon ma'am I'm right behind you." Remy reassured the woman as walked slowly backwards down the ladder. The lady tentatively put one foot after another as she slowly descended the siding.

"If I fall you'll catch me?" The old lady called down to Remy.

"Well I've got no choice, it's either that or we both go down in the water. We don't want that do we?" Remy asked.

"No, we sure don't." The lady came steadily down until Remy was able to take her into his arms and with Sugar Doll's help settle her into the boat.

"Lucky you a small little thing." Remy smiled. They untied the boat and pushed off to find shelter for the woman.

"Hey, how ya'll doin'?" A man yelled out in a passing boat. There were many people out helping with the rescue efforts.

"We're fine. Hey where can we take her to shelter?" Remy asked the man.

"There are several checkpoints that are taking folks to different Red Cross shelters. The Superdome is one place and the Convention Center is another but you are closer to Canal Street so you can take her to the police so that they can bring her somewhere safe.

"I want to go by my brother's house." The old lady chimed in at that moment.

"Where's that Miss?"

"Lake Charles." The old lady replied smiling.

"Well now dahling, you gonna have to see the authorities about that 'cause this little boat can't carry us that far." Remy winked at the woman.

"He's so kind." Sugar Doll thought to herself as she looked at her man in the light of day.

There were many people who needed rescuing, mostly elderly. Sugar Doll was exhausted by day's end. The heat was unbearable as they trudged back across Canal Street carrying the little canoe.

"Hey Remy!" A voice called out from across the street. Remy dropped his end of the boat and ran to embrace his friend.

"Man how you doin'? The tall ebony man asked as he hugged Remy in a long embrace.

"Good and you? Your family?" Remy asked concerned as he stepped away from the embrace.

"I don't know man. I can't find them. Everything across the river is devastated. I have to go to the Superdome next and it's packed with people man."

Sugar Doll approached the men slowly. "Baby, can you help me with the boat?" She asked tentatively.

"I'm sorry Sugar; this here is the famous drummer Eddie Haskins." Remy patted his friend on the shoulder.

"Hi Eddie." Sugar Doll said shyly.

"Hey there. You guys look like you made it through the hurricane all right." Eddie squinted."

"I still have to find my mother." Sugar Doll sighed."

"I know how you feel I need to find my wife and kids. I don't know where anybody is and all of the circuits are busy so I can't even call on the cell phone."

"Where do you think they are?" Sugar Doll asked.

"A lot of people went to the Superdome before the storm. I'm headed over there." Eddie related.

Sugar Doll looked at Remy.

"The streets over there are flooded but we've got this boat." Remy pointed to the boat that Sugar Doll had left behind on the median.

"Let's go man!" Eddie ran toward the little boat.

Sugar Doll and Remy ran behind him every inch of their body aching from all of the heavy lifting they had done during the day.

"Are you all right Patrice?" Elise asked for what seemed the hundredth time.

"Yes, please stop fussing over me! He scared me that was all. Thank you so much for not listening to me. I'm glad that you followed me." Patrice kissed her sister on the cheek. Elise grabbed her in an enormous bear hug.

"Where we going ya'll?" Bobby Joe asked.

"Somewhere far from here bro." Tommy answered. As they walked outside the heat hit them first. The sky was a clear blue and the sun was shining as though it had somehow been brought closer to the earth.

"God Damn it's hot!" Bobby Joe exclaimed.

"What's that smell?" Elise asked.

"It feels like an oven out here." Tommy said.

"Where are we going?" Patrice asked suddenly frightened.

"Well, wherever we go we are going to have to get wet." Bobby Joe said as he saw the water at a level of 3 feet.

Mona picked up her phone receiver again but was not surprised that she had no service.

"All circuits are busy." Droned from her cell phone as she tried to call Big Ma for the thousandth time. She hoped that Sugar Doll was safely in Gonzales.

"I want to take a look outside." Mona said to Mr. Renair.

"Be careful, I'm gonna stay put. Folks say the hurricane is dangerous. I say it's the time after that."

"Why do you say that?" Mona asked mildly alarmed.

"Well besides all of the infections and diseases you can catch, there are the looters and thieves out looking for an easy score. It's better if they don't know about you." Mr. Reniar sat back sipping his coffee.

Mona thought of her bar then. Would the French Quarters be protected? As she opened her front door she again saw the debris but not the severe amount of damage she'd heard reported on the radio. It must be in outlying areas.

"Several dead bodies have been found in New Orleans' East." The radio reported. Mona closed the door. The heat enveloped her. She wanted to open a window but they were all boarded up giving the house the effect of evening time.

"What are we going to do Mr. Renair? Mona asked.

"We wait, that's what. Wait until it's all over." Mr. Renair seemed to have a lot of time to wait.

Mona was restless and wanted to check on her bar. She resolved to go out to check on her place. As she changed into jeans and water boots she kept seeing Tony's face. "He's gone now, stop that." She cajoled herself.

Dauphine Street had mostly wind damage. To Mona it looked like Godzilla had walked through and blew down little things. Shingles, tree branches and glass littered the road and the sidewalk but none of it matched the horror she'd heard on the radio. She arrived at her bar with much less effort than she had had to walk home in the two nights before.

"Hey Mona, are you going to be open for business?" Benny greeted her with his usual friendliness.

"Now Benny, how am I going to do that with no power?" Mona smiled at her friend.

"A few people here have emergency generators. I could sure use a beer." Benny was an old regular resident of the Quarters.

"C'mon in and let's see what we can get for you." Mona invited Benny in as she took out her keys. They heard the noise as soon as they walked into the darkened bar.

"Hey someone's coming in!" Came an urgent whisper.

"Ssssh! Stupid!" The second voice warned.

Benny pushed Mona behind him.

"C'mon outta there, we can hear you." Benny called to the invaders.

Silence. "We are coming in and we are armed." Benny called again. Mona punched his shoulder.

"All right Mister, don't shoot. We were just hungry that's all." A young girl of about ten stepped out of the shadows.

"How did you get in here?" Mona yelled in spite of herself. There was a brief scrambling and then the sound of broken glass crunching under someone's feet. Mona moved quickly past the young girl to the back of the bar into the storage room. The service window stood broken and a small boy of about six years old was trying to climb out onto the street. His hands had blood on them.

"What are you doing?" Mona ran to the boy and grabbed him around the waist. She pulled him back into the room. He started to cry. She felt fists on her back.

"Leave him alone, he ain't doing you nothing!" Screamed the little girl.

Benny came quickly and picked her up as she kicked and screamed.

"Where did you kids come from?" Mona asked as she cleaned off the boy's hands. It looked as though he's just pounded his hands against the service window and cut both hands badly.

"Our mother died in the storm." The little girl offered.

"Oh?" Mona was shocked by this information.

"We had to swim and then this man gave us a ride to the police but they didn't have time for us so we came here." The girl continued.

"Why did you come here?" Mona asked.

"Our momma's name was Mona." The little girl cried. Mona's heart melted and she hugged the girl.

Mona went to the freezer and although it had been off for two days the food hadn't spoiled. She took out a few steak chops a container of potato salad and set about preparing a meal for the children. Benny was already at the bar having a beer.

"Are they still cold?" Mona asked not minding the idea of a cold one herself.

"They'll do." Benny said and handed her one.

ꕥ

Eddie, Sugar Doll and Remy guided the canoe toward the Superdome. The cars on the street were all flooded. People waded by them looking dazed and afraid. As they approached the Superdome the three passengers realized that they had taken on a huge task.

"We've got to come up with some sort of plan to divide up and find our family and friends. Remy suggested.

"Well, we can't leave the boat behind, somebody will steal it." Sugar Doll worried about getting back to the Quarters.

"I'm not leaving you behind." Remy said flatly.

"Maybe we can hide it somewhere." Eddie suggested. They began looking around for hiding spaces as soon as he'd said it.

There was a small space next to the dome which seemed abandoned. They stowed the boat there and waded into the water which was waist deep. The water did nothing to cool them off as it was as hot as the humid summer air. Eddie was anxious to see his family so he jogged ahead of Remy and Sugar Doll.

"Do we split up and meet back somewhere or what?" Sugar Doll asked.

"No dahling, we are going to stay together that's all. If we don't find her today we will find her in time. Don't worry." Remy comforted her.

"Mona probably doesn't know that the Quarters are safe again. Especially looking at all of this." Sugar Doll bit her lip.

"We'll find her." Remy said.

They approached the building with trepidation. Eddie had already disappeared into the building.

The building was hot, perhaps hotter than outside if that was possible.

"Hey man, you don't want to go in there man!" A young boy sat next to the entrance looking out hopefully.

"Thanks for the tip." Remy said as he took Sugar Doll's hand to lead her to the inside of the stadium.

They were unprepared for the mass of humanity there. People were everywhere. The stale unventilated air assaulted their noses. It would take a month to locate anyone in this building. They descended the first level of stairs looking on both aisles. They didn't have a photo of Mona to show so they had to depend on just seeing her. Remy glanced at Sugar Doll knowing that their chances of finding Mona in this mess were very low. As they ascended the stairs they noticed a particular trend. Many people who were from across the river had been there in one section at the beginning of the storm. The new arrivals were on the other side of the building.

"Yeah baby, if your momma came from Charity Hospital they probably have her on the other side of the building. We been here for a few days." A woman who sat with her five children told them. "I heard that they are getting buses to take us out of here before they run out of food and water. Luckily we brought our own." She nodded.

Sugar Doll thanked the woman and walked away.

As they walked toward the area with newcomers Sugar Doll saw someone in the distance who looked familiar. She touched Remy's arm.

"Do you see her?" Remy asked surprised.

"No, but I think I see one of the girls I came up here with. Let's go there to check; maybe they've seen my mother as well." Sugar Doll said hopefully. They ran back up the stairs toward the opening of the stadium.

"Elise?" Sugar Doll yelled as soon as she came out of the building. Both girls turned at the call.

"Sugar Doll!" They yelled in unison.

The girls ran to each other in an embrace.

"Girl we were worried about you. Did you go to your momma's?" Elise asked excitedly.

"Yes, but then I was at my..." Sugar Doll hesitated.

"She was at her boyfriend's house." Remy walked up behind her and kissed her on the neck.

"Oh, oh...look out!" Patrice laughed.

"You dating a white boy?" Elise blurted out."

"Elise!" Patrice admonished.

"It's all right, I am white." Remy laughed

"He's cute girl." Elise winked and managed to flash a smile at Bobby Joe.

Bobby Joe looked away.

"Where are ya'll going?" Sugar Doll asked.

"We were just asking ourselves that." Patrice said.

"Why don't you just stay here until they release people?" Sugar Doll asked.

"It's dangerous in there and hot and smelly. We were sitting next to a dead body of a girl. We have to bounce." Patrice said.

"A man attacked Patrice!" Elise blurted out.

"What?" Sugar Doll and Remy said in unison.

"I'm fine. Big Elise here fell on the man and the entire bathroom came to my rescue." Patrice rolled her eyes at Elise.

"He still attacked you." Elise said.

Remy and Sugar Doll exchanged a glance.

"Mona's in there." Sugar Doll said worried.

"You couldn't pay me money to go back." Patrice said.

"I heard that Gretna wasn't affected at all. If we can just get to the bridge we can all go over to my cousin's house in Harvey." Tommy piped up.

"We have to try to find Mona." Sugar Doll said sadly.

"Okay well we wish ya'll good luck." Bobby Joe said.

Patrice gave Sugar Doll another squeeze.

"I can't do it girl, I can't go back in there. I'm sorry."

"It's okay, I understand. Remy's apartment in the Quarters wasn't damaged. We'll go back there after we find her or get tired of looking."

"There's no electricity and from what I heard the water isn't safe to drink." Patrice said.

"We'll be all right for a few days until things clear up. We spent the day trying to help people get down off of their rooftops. If you ask me it's no better out in the city." Sugar Doll said.

People were passing them wading through the water trying to make it back to their homes.

"Okay, but there's one way to find out. Let's go." Tommy said.

"Be careful." Patrice warned Sugar Doll.

"I will." Sugar Doll promised. The friends parted ways. Remy took Sugar Doll's hand and they went back into the Superdome to look for Mona.

"Our momma couldn't swim." Shonda told Mona. "She sent us to swim classes since we were babies but never had the time to learn herself." She cried.

"You don't have to talk about it." Mona said as she cleared away the plates.

"What's your brother's name? He hasn't said a word." Mona asked.

"John." Came the simple answer.

The children had been through a lot. Mona felt something she wasn't used to feeling, pity.

"Well, I'm going back to my apartment and wait for the power to come on honey." Benny said rising to leave.

"All right Benny, you've been good company. Come back to-morrow if you get bored. I might need your help." Mona smiled.

"Why sure. The job ain't there no mo' so I'm available and at your service…for a beer or two." He winked and walked out of the door.

"Good ole Benny." Mona smiled. He had been a regular customer for years.

"Ya'll want to come to my house until we can find your relatives?" Mona asked.

"Yes." Shonda smiled knowing that she had made the right choice.

Mona walked over to the broken service window that Bernie had boarded up. She swept up the glass into a bin, dusted off her skirt and locked up the back area of the bar.

"Let's go kids." Mona said.

She hadn't been a mother in years. It felt good.

"Miss Jones, can you come by our rooms please." Pastor Han spoke into the phone. Big Ma's heart raced. What could it be?

She rushed toward his rooms.

"My cousin just came back from flying over the Parish. James why don't you tell her what you saw." Pastor Han motioned for Big Ma to sit down.

James was a tall, powerfully built young man. He was young and handsome. He had a kind look in his eyes.

"Well ma'am like I was telling my cousin, it's bad. The entire town is decimated, gone, and our little neighborhood is unrecognizable. The only reason I knew where I was because of the radar and latitude. There were 30 foot waves that just took everything. There were a few boats stacked against each other and the bridge is still intact but the town is just…well… gone."

It was late evening when Big Ma received the news that all of lower Plaquemines Parish had been devastated. There was nothing left. Her little house by the river was gone. Her husband had built that house with his own hands.

Chapter Seventeen

"Sugar, let's go back to my apartment. We aren't going to find her here. She may have gone somewhere else." Remy suggested after the third level of searching bore no results.

"You're right. Let's go. I'm tired and we still have to wade through that mess. I just want to go and clean off and sleep." Sugar Doll agreed.

They made their way back through the crowded Superdome. As they left the building they saw that their boat had remained untouched. Grateful that that was the case Remy jumped into the water and waded through it to retrieve the boat. Sugar Doll waited gratefully on the steps. Every inch of her body ached. Remy paddled toward her resigned to the thought that it would probably be impossible to find Mona until the storm was over. Eddie had disappeared into the Superdome and they hadn't seen him since.

"Let's go honey." She straddled onto the back part of the boat and hugged Remy from behind. She felt relief and comfort as she leaned her head against his back.

More people were out wading through the water. It was obvious that no help had arrived as more people swarmed on the Superdome. It was no better than where they had come from.

"I'm glad that I have somewhere to go." She whispered to Remy as they passed a woman and child wearing tattered clothes.

"Me too Sugar, me too." Remy pulled her arm tightly around his chest.

They finally made it to Canal Street which had blockades set up and uniformed police officers on patrol.

"They must be guarding the Quarter." Remy said. He dragged the canoe like an obedient dog behind him. Sugar Doll nudged closer to him as she realized that somehow New Orleans was under martial law.

"Sir, you gonna have to turn back. The Quarters are closed for business. Haven't you heard? We've done had ourselves a hurricane." The first police officer said.

"I…we…live in the Quarters. We just went out to try to find her mama." Remy said politely.

"Ah, that's nice but I'm not allowed to allow anyone to come through here." The officer said.

"I have my driver's license here proving my residence." Remy took out his wallet.

"Let me see it." The officer said. Remy handed over the license.

"Okay, I'll let you pass but you shouldn't try to come out after this. The mayor will be setting up a curfew. The city is closed for business and anybody out here is probably up to no good." The officer looked sternly at both Sugar Doll and Remy.

They walked carefully past him. "Hey, where are they going?" Another officer yelled out so they quickened their pace.

"I never thought I'd have to make a run for it to go to my own apartment." Remy laughed.

"We've already been given permission to go why are we running?" Sugar Doll asked already out of breath.

"Just in case." Remy said as he looked over his shoulder to see the officer conferring with the one who had released them. He slowed his pace and grabbed Sugar Doll's arm.

"They've stopped." They both breathed a sigh of relief as they walked slowly toward the Quarters.

They entered Remy's apartment exhausted from the day.

"Well Sugar it looks like our water supply is nil." Remy said as he tried the faucet but there was no running water.

"I've got one gallon of water under the sink and a half gallon in the fridge." He joked.

"I'm a typical bachelor, my food supply is terrible." He rubbed his stomach as he looked in the bare cabinet. There was one lonesome can of tuna in the corner of the cupboard.

"I just want to sleep." Sugar Doll sighed as she headed for the bedroom. She took off her soaked jeans and fell hard onto the unmade bed.

"Now that's a beautiful picture." Remy sighed as he removed his pants and shirt.

"Don't even think about it." Sugar Doll smiled sleepily into the pillow.

"Now that's impossible. I am going to think about it, I'm just not going to do anything about it...yet." Remy pulled Sugar Doll to his body and they curled into a peaceful sleep.

Big Ma watched the news and saw the lack of response the government was giving to the people. "Lord, Lord, what's going to happen now?" She lamented as she reached for her bible. Pastor

Han and his wife tried to comfort her but they had lost everything as well. Their entire way of life was changed forever.

"Well, ma'am the one thing we all have is the good sense that God gave to us. We all have insurance." Pastor Han tried to ease the dark mood of the room. His wife cried silently in the corner.

"Those poor people still stuck in the city with no food and water. It's a terrible shame. It feels like we are in a third world country with no one to protect us." Big Ma cried.

"I hate to say it but I think that because New Orleans is predominantly black the help is going to continue to be slow in coming." Pastor Han said.

"We still human. Don't the people see the people suffering? What about the little children? There are dead bodies in the water for God's sake!" Big Ma said becoming upset.

"Now calm yourself Big Ma. There ain't nothing we can do about it now. We know that our love ones are safe and sound and that's all we can do. We can pray for America to see how they are treating us and then God will make a move." Pastor Han began in his preacher's voice.

"Oh Lord, Lord. Why have you forsaken us?" Big Ma cried. She felt a familiar pain down her left arm. It happened so quickly that she hadn't noticed the warning signs. She went down on one knee, her mouth drooping to the side.

"Mrs. Jones! Mrs. Jones!" Pastor Han yelled alarmed. His wife jumped into action going to Big Ma and helping her down to the floor. Her eyes rolled back into her head.

"Call an ambulance! Call an ambulance! NOW!" She screamed.

Mona returned to the house where Mr. Renair was waiting. He had cooked a dinner of catfish and rice.

"Oh I see that you've brought company with you." Mr. Renair smiled.

"Hi Mr. Renair, this is Shonda and her little brother John." Mona introduced the pair.

"Pleased to meet you. Are ya'll hungry?" Mr. Renair asked.

"No sir, we already ate at Mona's." Shonda answered. John hid behind his sister.

"We've already eaten." Mr. Renair corrected.

"Oh, you ate too?" Shonda asked.

"No, pardon me; I have 35 years of teaching experience that makes me correct children. My apologies." Mr. Renair smiled.

Shonda looked at him confused and then shrugged.

"You've sure got a big house." Shonda said.

"It's not that big but it's nice. There is a room upstairs if you guys are tired you can go upstairs and take a nap." Mona said.

"Thank you Miss Mona." John spoke up for the first time.

"Just go to the first room at the top of the stairs." Mona directed.

"Yes ma'am. Shonda and John said in unison.

They ran up the stairs.

"Nice kids, relatives of yours?" Mr. Renair asked.

"No, they aren't. They broke into the bar. Their mother drowned in the storm and they found my place and were hiding." Mona said sadly.

"How traumatic. Are they okay?" Mr. Renair asked.

"No, I don't think they are. When this all blows over I'll try to help them to find their relatives. Hopefully the power will come back on soon. I have an old generator out back. I may need your help in turning it on." Mona said.

"I'm your man." Mr. Renair smiled finding a new found respect for his neighbor.

Sugar Doll woke up first. Remy was tangled in the sheets next to her. "He's taken all of the bed coverings". She thought to herself. It was just as well as the room was blazing. She kissed his shoulder and he moaned. She was very thirsty. She went to the kitchen to get a glass of water and then remembered that Remy was short on supply. She poured herself a half glass and drank it down slowly like one would a fine wine. She couldn't believe that she was here, in the midst of a storm. Her life had definitely taken a turn.

"Good morning." Remy had crept up behind her. She jumped startled at first but then leaned into his sexy embrace.

"Good morning honey." Sugar Doll smiled. He kissed her on the neck.

"Good morning. I wish I had a cup of coffee to offer you." Remy smiled apologetically.

"What else do you have to offer me?" Sugar Doll looked suggestively at Remy.

"Don't tempt me. We decided to wait didn't we?" He smiled as he quickly lifted her and carried her off to the bedroom.

"I know but now I am regretting that decision." She sighed.

"Don't." He dropped her on the bed playfully. "Things are too unsettled now and I want you to know that I wouldn't take advantage of you just because you are stuck with me." He backed away from the bed.

"I'm not stuck with you. I wanted to be here." She sat up on the bed's edge.

"All the same, when this thing is over we can think more about our relationship and where it's headed. You are special to me." Remy smiled and sat down next to her.

"Can we kiss then?" She asked innocently.

"Let's go back to the living room, far away from temptation." He took her hand and led her away into the outer room and embraced her in a warm kiss.

"I think I love you Sugar Doll." Remy breathed in her hair.

"I love you too." Sugar Doll allowed herself to say the very thing she'd always been afraid of. She'd remained a virgin for so long because her trust had died. Her trust died with her father and her mother's abandonment. "I'm afraid, but I love you." She admitted as he caressed her face.

"You should never be afraid of me. I will never leave you baby. I will always love you. Trust in me." Remy's bright blue eyes looked into hers and she knew that she was his forever.

Big Ma slipped into a netherworld in which everything was bright. She was fourteen again. She was walking along the levee on a warm summer's day. The clover was in full bloom. She walked to meet a friend. She saw him sitting on the river's bank sipping a cup of coffee. She could smell the rich scent quite clearly and decided she wanted some too. She approached her friend; his face was unusually bright and happy. He opened his red thermos and handed her a little plastic cup. He poured the strong chicory coffee into the cup.

"Now hold on a minute, I know you like cream in your coffee and a little sugar too." Her friend said and he opened a bag with half and half and a pound of sugar. He took out his spoon and stirred it into her cup and handed it to her. She settled into the soft green clover of the levee and an unexpected cool breeze washed over them both.

"Now this is living." Big Ma said as she sipped her coffee and poked Bertrand in the side. They both let out a giggle and enjoyed the view of the lazy Mississippi as it passed them by on its way to the city.

The ambulance finally arrived. Big Ma's entire left side was contorted now. She was unable to talk. She seemed to be smiling. Pastor Han looked over at his wife as they loaded Mrs. Jones into the ambulance and they both knew. He climbed into the ambulance clutching the bible.

The sound of glass breaking woke Remy from his peaceful sleep. The sun shone through the cracks in the boards he had against the windows. He jumped up to see what was going on downstairs. The drugstore across the street was surrounded by people who were breaking out the windows. Remy peeked through the bay windows he had recently de-boarded. He glanced over at Sugar Doll who remained sleeping peacefully.

"Things are going to get bad." He said under his breath as the realization of it sent his heart racing.

"I've got to get Sugar Doll out of the city." He mumbled as he saw that the people had successfully broken through the glass. He went back to the bed but decided to allow her to sleep. The way her brow furrowed in her sleep made him smile.

"I'm gone man, gone." Remy smiled to himself and playfully kissed her on the forehead. He decided to go downstairs to find out what the locals were doing. He didn't get far when he saw Benny walking toward him carrying a shotgun.

"Man where you going with that thing… deer hunting?" Remy asked half joking yet mildly alarmed.

"No man, the looters are out in force and I've got to protect my place. It's about to get dangerous in the Quarters. The city is shut down and no help is coming either." Benny looked over at the drugstore as it was being looted.

"Are there any evacuation areas out of the city?" Remy asked.

"What the floods haven't blocked the police are. I heard that at a few of the hotels people are paying for a charter bus out of the city." Benny pointed down the street. "Get out man; I'm only staying to protect my business." Benny walked away. Remy stood on the street looking as the people were climbing through the windows. The sound of glass cracking pervaded the whole street. He raced up the stairs to get Sugar Doll. She was already sitting up in bed.

"Baby we've got to get out of the city. The police are really not around and the worst elements are showing their faces." Remy said as he grabbed his small suitcase which stood already packed on the dresser.

"I thought that you said that we would be safe in the Quarter's." Sugar Doll admonished but rose up quickly.

"I thought we would be but I didn't think that the storm would be as bad as it was. There is no running water in the city and the government isn't giving us any help right now. People are getting desperate. We need to try to evacuate. I want to get to the car but I need to find out which routes are available for travel." He turned the transistor radio on but heard only static.

"Let's just go. We'll find a way out of the city. Things are only going to get worse."

Chapter Eighteen

Patrice, Bobby Joe, Elise and Tommy all banded together as they walked onto the expressway. People littered the bridge. It didn't even look like the city bridge. Some people lay on blankets sleeping while others fed their children from baby food jars. Elise pressed closer to Patrice. "Why are they just staying here on the bridge?" She asked aloud.

"I guess they ain't got nowhere else to go." Tommy said. There were young people holding up signs asking for water.

"I'm scared Patrice." Elise said.

"Me too. Let's just keep walking." Patrice suggested.

"Where are we going to go?" Elise asked.

"My cousin's house in Harvey." Tommy suggested. "Ya'll welcome until this blows over and you find your family. They walked through the people on the bridge oddly separated from them. They had a look of determination and some people began to follow them. When they reached the highest point of the bridge Bobby Joe could see that up ahead there were several police cars at the bottom.

"Look ya'll, they must be there to help people!" He shouted for joy as he broke into a fast run. The growing crowd of followers began to run behind him. Patrice and Elise kept pace.

As they drew closer to the blockade one of the sheriffs spoke to them on the megaphone: "Now listen! Ya'll cannot pass!

Gretna will not be New Orleans! Go back to where you came from. You can't pass here!"

Stunned the crowd of fifty or more people crowded in behind their new leader Bobby Joe. "Ya'll can't stop us from going to our families." He shouted.

"The hell we can't!" The sheriff shouted. "Now turn around!" He cocked his rifle and shot into the air. The crowd was stunned and began to turn back. Five of the police officers also pulled their guns and shot above their heads.

"Tell the rest of them." The sheriff shouted as the crowd began to run.

Patrice ran as hard as she could, crying all the while. Elise ran behind her but her face was devoid of any emotion.

"What's going on when the police shoot at you for trying to go home?" Bobby Joe asked.

They slowed their running when they had managed a safe distance from the police.

"Man, this is crazy! Now where we gonna go?" Tommy asked as he held onto the bridge railing.

"Elise! Elise!" Patricia screamed as Elise fell to the ground.

"Too much running." Bobby Joe joked as he walked over to the girls.

Tommy approached them but saw the red stain on Elise's left side. He dropped down to her side.

"She's been shot!" Tommy shouted. A few people approached to see what was going on.

"Them peckerwoods shot her!" Tommy screamed.

Patricia grabbed Elise's heavy body in her arms. The young girl was unconscious.

"Help! Help!" Bobby Joe screamed aloud.

❦

"Mr. Renair, I'm going to go back to my bar to make sure that everything is locked down. I'm worried about what's going on in the Quarters." Mona said as she tied her shoes.

"Do you think it's wise to go back out there?" Mr. Renair asked.

"No one is going to do me anything. People are desperate for food and water. Maybe I can help and save my bar." Mona said as she walked out of the door.

❦

Sugar Doll and Remy walked to his car and threw in their stuff.

"Let's go see if Mona went back to the bar before we leave." Sugar Doll suggested.

"You think she's there?" Remy asked.

"I can't imagine Mona staying at the Superdome. Her car is still in the alley behind her bar." Sugar Doll shrugged.

"Good point." Remy smiled. "Let's go." He turned the car around and headed for Royal Street. There were crowds of people breaking into the drugstore to get food.

"Wow that's scary." Sugar Doll exclaimed.

"Yeah but it's been three days since the storm hit and there is no running water or supplies. What else are people supposed to do?" Remy lamented.

"Some of the people are so poor and really have nowhere to go. You'd think if the government can help all of those other countries when they suffer from disasters they can help right here at home." Sugar Doll said angrily while Remy nodded in agreement.

They pulled up to the entrance of Royal Street. Three teenaged boys were roaming around looking into windows for the next place to break into as one carried a small portable television. Remy felt ashamed of them.

"It's one thing to loot for food and water but damned!" He said under his breath.

He leaned into the car window, "Stay in the car and close the window." He instructed Sugar Doll. She felt frightened for him. The boys drew closer.

"What the hell you looking at white boy?" One of the boys said.

"Nothing." Remy said with meaning holding the younger boy's gaze.

"I thought not." He said and the other boys giggled with glee. Remy walked past them. They stared after him but soon lost interest as they spotted an antique store down the street.

Remy walked tenuously toward the bar. The bright green neon sign which read Mona's was broken and a few of the front windows were broken but the bars on the main window had blocked hopeful looters. Remy looked up and down the street. He went to the back of the building to yell up at the window again. Mona's car remained in the alleyway packed up to the roof.

"Mona! Mona!" He yelled up at the window.

"What you hollering at boy?" Benny rounded the corner.

"I'm looking for a friend." Remy answered.

"Who?" Benny asked suspiciously.

"My girlfriend's mother." Remy answered.

"What's her name? I might know her, I live right up there." Benny pointed to the apartments across the street.

"Mona." Remy answered.

"Oh, Mona ain't here, she's at her house on Dauphine Street. I just saw her last night." Benny answered.

"Really?" Remy said getting excited.

"Benny's the name. Tell her that I helped you out. I didn't know she had a daughter though."

"Thank you sir." Remy shook the man's hand and took off running.

"Tell her that Benny helped you!" He shouted after the boy laughing. He looked forward to another free beer.

Remy was strangely relieved that Mona was still in the French Quarters. He ran happily toward Sugar Doll in the car.

"Remy!" Sugar Doll's voice pierced the air.

As he approached the car he saw that the young boys he'd passed had broken the car window and were trying to pull Sugar Doll out of it. Remy felt his blood run hot. He broke into a sprint toward the car. He ran toward the biggest boy who was tearing at Sugar Doll's blouse. An animalistic grunt escaped his mouth as he pushed the boy into the window's broken glass. He released Sugar Doll yelping as he felt the sting of the broken glass in his side. The other two boys came to the aid of their friend and jumped Remy with full force. Remy was like a released bull scrapping with the boy who was unsuccessfully trying to pin his arm. He heard the car door open.

"Sugar Doll! Stay in the car! Stay in the car!" He ordered. He heard another yelping sound and then the crush of the three young men lightened. He fought the remaining boy who was no more than fifteen years old. He clocked one swift right hook to his cheek. The boy fell out cold. He looked up to see Benny kicking another boy who took off into a swift run. Sugar Doll leaned against the door of the car shaken with sprinkles of blood on her white blouse.

"You alright?" Remy asked jumping to his feet.

She shook her head yes. Benny stooped down to look at the young boy close up.

"I know these boys. Trash." He spat.

"Thank you man." Remy grasped Benny's hand to shake it.

"Don't thank me, thank *her,* man. She knocked that boy down with the car door. I'm surprised he could still run after that." He chuckled amused. "I just gave him the extra kick to get him on his way.

Sugar Doll smiled at Remy who turned to her to give her a strong and emotional embrace. "When I saw him with his hands on you I thought that I would lose my mind." He kissed her urgently. She softened at his touch.

"I know when I'm not needed." Benny backed away smiling.

Mona walked through the French Quarter and she felt a sense of fear she had never had in the Quarters before. She heard the sirens of police cars and car alarms going off. There were people standing in clutters whispering in hushed voices. The street was darkened as the power was out and there was an eerie feeling in the air. Mona thought of her favorite novel and wondered if the Vampire LeStat was roaming around somewhere. She got a giggle at that thought and felt a bit more at ease.

"Funny that a vampire would actually make me feel safe." She thought to herself. "These are my streets. My home and no one is going to mess with me." She thought bravely even as she passed groups of people breaking into a store. As she drew closer to her bar she saw that the windows had been broken but the inner bars had prevented anyone getting into the business. She looked up and down the street debating whether she should open the gate or return to the safety of her house. Just as she turned toward her house she heard a loud whoop.

"Mona! Mona!" someone shouted from behind her. Benny came running toward her.

"Your daughter's still here." He smiled triumphantly.

"What are you talking about?" Mona felt her heart sink. Just then Sugar Doll walked from around the corner with Remy on her arm. There was blood on her blouse.

"What happened to you?" Mona shrieked instantly alarmed.

"She wrestled an alligator." Remy tried to make light of the moment.

Sugar Doll ran to her mother and hugged her crying. Mona cried as well unprepared for this level of emotion from her daughter.

"What happened?" her voice softened.

"Some guys tried to attack her, but we took care of them." Benny supplied.

"Yeah thanks man." Then turning to Mona and said, "This man deserves a beer." Remy supplied.

Mona stood hugging her daughter, "What are you still doing here?" she asked.

"We got stuck because of all of the road closings." Sugar Doll lied.

"Your grandmother's probably worried sick." Mona said.

"Yes, but I can't get through. All of the circuits are busy."

"That's not all, the city has gone crazy. It feels like we are the only ones left on the planet." Mona sighed. She continued to hug Sugar Doll relishing the feeling.

"Mona," Sugar Doll came out of the embrace, "We went to Charity Hospital. We know about Tony." She grimaced as she said his name because even though her hatred of the man ran deep she still felt empathy for her mother. Whatever else the man was he had been close to Mona.

"I can't talk about that." Mona said feeling her throat tightening up. The two walked back toward the bar amidst the darkening night sky. Remy came over to Sugar Doll and hugged her from behind. The feeling of love was palpable. Mona studied her daughter. She could see the look in her eyes and knew that she had given herself to the boy. They walked together toward Mona's house.

Patrice held her sister in her arms. Elise's breathing was heavy and labored. There was a strange rattle to it. There were people surrounding both girls but Patrice only heard the sound of her sister's breathing. She could feel her skin which had become cold and clammy. She placed her hand on the side of her cheek. She knew that the death rattle signified the beginning of the end. Someone was talking to her but she wanted to stay in that moment. She wanted to be there when Elise's spirit left her body. She needed to be there in that singular moment as she had been with her mother. The silence was deafening. The breathing came in and out, in and out. The breathing slowed and became deeper in sound. Patrice opened her eyes and looked at Elise and she blew out a final breath. She did it like one preparing to swim. Her head fell to the side and she was gone. Patrice let out a wail as she held her sister. Bobby Joe and Tommy stood behind her crying silently and in shock. The crowd that surrounded them began to walk away as though somehow the moment was too private to witness.

Chapter Nineteen

Remy held Sugar Doll in his arms as Reverend Han talked to her quietly. "Mrs. Jones had a smile on her face and I must say that she looked very peaceful." He wiped a tear from his cheek. His wife stood behind him patting him on the back. They were the consoling brigade. She knew that he'd looked to Mrs. Jones as a mother figure. She felt his deep sadness as well.

"Thank you Reverend." Sugar Doll managed to say. She fell into Remy's arms crying inconsolably. There would be no funeral in the lower Parish as it had been devastated by the horrific winds and water of Hurricane Katrina.

"We've lost so many, Sugar Doll. I want to go down to bless the ground but unfortunately they are still finding bodies." Reverend Han stepped back wiping his brow. He was devastated himself. He knew that life would never be the same.

"And Bertrand?" Sugar Doll asked.

A deep furrow appeared on the Reverend's brow. Mona had told him the details of the robbery. "Well, you know about our young misguided Kevin. Mrs. Han and I always tried to intercede with the boy and your grandmother too but we couldn't do enough. He got killed trying to do the devil's work. We can only pray that it's not as your mother has said." Reverend Han sighed.

"Bertrand would never be involved in a robbery. He had his own business, his own place. Why would he do something like that? Why would my mother say something like that?" Sugar Doll became freshly angered when she thought of it.

"Sugar, you've had enough bad news for today. Let's go back to the apartment to decide what you are going to do about your grandmother's funeral." Remy offered.

"It seems that this hurricane brought only death and murder with it." Sugar Doll cried.

"That poor young girl Elise…dying like that on the bridge." Mrs. Han lamented.

"They just shot randomly at people, like they were animals." Sugar Doll said.

"Sugar Doll, let's go." Remy wanted to take her away from all of the pain. He grasped her shoulder and led her to St. Peter's street. The French Quarters were in remarkably good condition after the storm. They had remained at Mona's house on Dauphine after the storm until things looked like they had blown over and each day brought fresh pain.

"Oh Remy, it's too much to handle." Sugar Doll said as they walked slowly back to his tiny flat.

"I know honey but we will…together." He smiled weakly, even losing some of his own spirit of mirth in the sadness.

Marsalas sat in his offices in the ice cold air conditioned room which was his true home. He gave orders in this room. He gave orders of who would live and who would die.

"I want my money. It's only a matter of time before Bertrand shows his face. I know that he wasn't smart enough to pull off something like that on his own." Marsalas said to Sid his right hand man. Sid's job was to agree and to execute orders.

"He was pretty tight with that singer kid Remy." Sid offered.

"I know and Remy is getting awfully cozy with Mona's daughter Sugar Doll." Marsalas said.

"You think that they had something to do with Tony's death, they are kind of young to come up with something like that." Sid asked.

"I don't put nothing past nobody." Marsalas answered.

"I've never trusted Mona. She has reasons of her own to want to kill Tony. I told him to be careful with that but he wanted her and you can't talk to a man when he's reasoning with his dick." Marsalas shrugged. He knew that he minimized what Tony had felt for Mona because his nephew had no business loving some nigger woman. He had to keep up appearances for the family.

"What you want me to do boss?" Sid asked.

"Wait. They ain't going nowhere. Too much media coverage with all of this aftermath stuff. Wait a few weeks and then I want you to start making inquiries. See if the kid is spending money he don't have. I'll handle Mona myself." He thought of all of the delicious ways he would handle her.

❦

The funeral was held in the city. Big Ma would have wanted to be buried in the Parish she loved but it was gone. The small town which had been her home was only so much rubble. Even though many had evacuated to different cities the funeral was standing room only. Somehow the grapevine had told everyone to come. That one of their beloved had left the earth and deserved to be honored. The woman who had fed those who didn't have a mother, prayed with those who had lost a husband or a child and wept with those who had lost a loved one in battle was gone. People from all walks of life came to the tiny funeral home. They had had to extend the visitation because people kept pouring in to wish their final goodbye. Little Tommy was all grown up and in uniform having heard about Big Ma's death while he was on leave from Iraq. He and Sugar Doll embraced and cried. The one person who was surprisingly absent was Bertrand.

"Where is he?" Sugar Doll asked Remy who was holding her hand as she scanned the room for her larger than life cousin. Remy didn't ask who she was talking about, he knew.

"Something's wrong" Sugar Doll worried. "No one's heard from him in weeks. That's not like him." She looked at Remy. As the procession left the funeral home for the burial ground the somber occasion took a lightened turn as Brophy played "When the Saints go Marching In". The crowd of mourners began the slow and steady second line. Big Ma would have liked that Sugar Doll smiled to herself.

"Any sign of that fat fuck?" Marsalas asked.

"No boss, no sign. We looked all over and waited before and after the funeral to catch sight of them." Sid answered.

"Well one thing them niggers love is their mammies and a good cry at the funeral. If he wasn't there he ain't in the state. Put feelers out in Biloxi and Florida. He'll turn up to his old stumping grounds sooner or later." Marsalas was becoming impatient with waiting.

❦

"I'm going to wait another week before opening the club again." Mona said as she sat on her couch still dressed in black from the funeral. She felt tired and defeated. Big Ma's death had hit her like a blow to the stomach. They had never gotten along but she was mama and now that person was gone. She felt all of her fifty-five years even if she looked twenty-five.

Mr. Renair rose and patted her on the hand. He saw the grief there and decided to give her time alone. "You know your momma's in heaven?" He asked innocently.

"Yes, that I do know Mr. Renair. But where will I go when I die? I could never be what she wanted me to be." Mona cried softly.

"Honey I have children too and the fact that you are is enough. She loved you. That's all you need to know." He gave her a fatherly pat on the head and walked to the door. He thought of his own mother then and tears came to his eyes. It was funny but he was nearly eighty years old and he still cried for her at times like this.

The atmosphere at Tony's funeral had been the opposite of Big Ma. Marsalas sat in the front and had all but sneered at Mona when she stooped to view the body. "He was handsome." Mona thought the familiar rush of sexual tension he inspired in her causing her to blush. "I'll miss you honey." She whispered as she bent to kiss his cheek. She felt a strong hand grasp her and pull her back. It was one of Marsala's men. She walked backwards down the aisle of the funeral home. She thought of leaving but she decided to take a seat at the back of the church. She had spent nearly twenty years with this man. She didn't share his final hour but the grief hit her hard now and she couldn't bear to leave the room. "Maybe he did have something to do with Kurt's death" she thought but she realized that she no longer cared. She realized that it was an excuse. She realized that she'd used that thought to keep the distance between him and her. She used it like a wedge to survive yet still she had loved him. When the priest closed the coffin she cried bitterly, like she'd never cried before.

Marsalas studied her, "Tears of guilt." He thought and planned to have her killed before the week was done. Tony was a lady's man and a gambler but he was his nephew and one of the few Marsalas could truly trust. His death left him alone with men who only wanted his position and knew nothing of loyalty, "Oh yes, that bitch has got to die." He thought vengefully as the procession left the church and headed for the cemetery.

"Mr. Marsalas has asked that you respect the family and not come to the burial site. We want to keep this in the family." Sid leaned down to whisper in Mona's ear.

"I am family." Mona said through her tears.

"No you ain't kid and that's final. Don't come. You ain't welcome." Sid put his burley hand on her shoulder and pressed her to the seat.

Mona sat still for awhile as the feeling of grief was replaced by outrage. She looked at the crucifix and waited as the final mourners left the church. She sat there in the silence of the church. "They think that I had something to do with Tony's death." She knew then that she had to leave New Orleans for good.

"We've got to find Bertrand." Sugar Doll cried into Remy's shoulder.

"Where would he go? Do you know that?" Remy asked her.

"Well, he usually vacations in Biloxi so that he can gamble. We really don't have any relatives out of state. We have a cousin in Atlanta." Sugar Doll sat up on the bed.

"Do you have his number?" Remy asked already reaching for the phone.

"Her number and yes." Sugar Doll felt a rush of relief as the thought of finding Bertrand became a possibility. She went to her purse on the nightstand and retrieved her address book.

"I don't know why I hadn't thought of this before. Carla is a distant cousin but I do recall Bertrand saying that he was going to visit her just last year." She took out the number as Remy handed her the phone.

The phone rang several times until she reached an answering machine, "This is Carla…you know what to do." Carla's friendly voice rang out and made Sugar Doll smile in spite of her concern for Bertrand.

"Hey girl, this is your cousin Sugar Doll in New Orleans. We are all alright but I haven't heard from Bertrand and I was wondering if he came out your way? Give me a call on my cell to let me know if you have heard anything." She hung up disappointed but hopeful. Remy pulled her close. They had been through a lot together and he hated to see the pain on her face.

"Hey dahling, cheer up! Tonight is the grand re-opening of Mona's and we're singing there." He smiled. Sugar Doll smiled reluctantly as well. It seemed that Tony had gotten what he'd wanted. Bertrand's club Beauchamp's sat dark and closed.

"It has been three weeks; we should file a missing person's report." Sugar Doll sat up out of Remy's arms.

"Honey the sheriff's department is so busy with all of the devastation that they are not even going to pay attention to that claim. Besides there are thousands of missing person's reports. Many people simply left the state to evacuate for the hurricane. That's what they are going to assume about Bertrand." Remy shrugged.

"That doesn't mean that we shouldn't do anything. Even if it takes time it's better that we have some record of looking for him. Something may be wrong. It's not like him not to call or contact me or someone else in the family. We all have each other's numbers. I was numb after Big Ma died but I know for a fact that she wouldn't just let this thing go. We have got to find him and we have got to try to find him!" Sugar Doll stood up determined to do something.

"I understand how you feel honey. I didn't want to worry you but I already put in a missing person's report but they told me what I just told you...basically that he'll turn up." Remy offered.

"Well thank you for that. Why didn't you tell me?" Sugar Doll asked.

"I didn't want to worry you with all else you were going through and I thought that they would come up with something before now but I see that is not going to happen." Remy went over to hug Sugar Doll.

"I can't help but feel that something bad has happened. I'm worried about him." Sugar Doll cried.

"I know honey, I know." Just then the phone rang.

"Hello cuz!" Came the bubbly voice of Carla. "What up?"

"That was fast." Sugar Doll sighed a breath of relief.

"Chow, I'm at the barber's. I got my hair cut to the quick honey and I love it!" Carla smiled into the phone.

"Cool...listen Carla, I'm calling about something serious." Sugar Doll interrupted.

"What's the matter?" Carla became immediately alarmed.

"Well, I don't know yet but no one has heard from Bertrand since the hurricane. He didn't come to Big Ma's funeral. That's just not like him."

"Yes, I heard about it. I'm sorry I couldn't come either, funds were tight. I'm surprised about Bertrand. He loved Big Ma the most." Carla said.

"So you haven't heard from him either?" Sugar Doll asked feeling the disappointment seep into her toes.

"No girl, I can't think of the last time I did talk to Bertie. I hope he's all right. Let me know when you hear anything. This hurricane has everyone all mixed up and confused. He probably just evacuated to another city and hasn't had time to call." Carla offered.

"It's just not like him. My mother said that he was supposed to pick me up down home but I ended up coming up with the Sheriff." Sugar Doll sat down on the bed.

"Have you filed a missing person's report?" Carla asked.

"My boyfriend did a few weeks back but they said that they were backed up and it was not possible to give an immediate response." Sugar Doll's voice cracked.

"Go check back and call me back this evening." Carla said finally.

Sugar Doll hung up the phone feeling completely defeated.

"Sugar, let's get out of here and get ready for tonight's gig. That should cheer you up." He walked to the closet and pulled out the beautiful gown he'd purchased for her.

"Oh Remy! How wonderful! I love this. No one has ever done this for me." Sugar Doll jumped up with glee.

"Before we go do you think that we could go down to the sheriff's office and just check? It would make me feel better." Sugar Doll asked as she hugged the dress closely to her waist.

"I don't see why not. Go and get dressed. Give those policemen something to think about. They'll probably help you faster after seeing you in that dress, cher." Remy gave her an affection kiss on the cheek.

"Yeah boss I'm right in front of the apartment. The girl is a real looker. They look like they are headed for the club." Sid spoke into the tiny flip phone as he sipped his coffee. It was too bitter for his taste but it woke up his senses. This type of work was well beneath him but his boss had taken a personal interest. If it was personal for his boss, then it was personal for him. He slowly edged the black sedan away from the curb as he followed the light blue Cadillac the kid drove.

As Remy looked for parking around the Sheriff's department he noticed the same black sedan that had passed the street three times. He assumed that the driver was looking for parking but there was an odd tugging feeling in his gut so he gave the car a direct look and made eye contact with the driver. The older man became flustered and drove off.

"The kid made me. They went into the police office. I don't know boss, if they were holding stolen money they wouldn't go courting the police to my thinking." Sid spoke into the phone.

"I don't pay you to think. I pay you to find out information. I've got two cops down there on the payroll. Go to the Esplanade Mall in fifteen minutes and one of them will come to tell you what the kids were looking for in the first place."

ꕥ

The sheriff of lower Plaquemines Parish scratched his head. The road block which separated the parish from onlookers was still in place. "If you ask me this whole thing is just a pain in the ass." He spoke to his deputy who nodded silently in agreement. The clean-up was under way and there were construction crews coming in by the truck load.

"How in the hell are we supposed to tell the looters from the workers?" The Sheriff spoke mostly to himself.

"The bulldozers are easy to inspect but the rest of this crap... well, no disrespect but most of your lower parish was trailers anyway. There wasn't really anything of value down there." The deputy shrugged.

A large truck pulled to the side of the road right before the roadblock, "Excuse me your officers. I thought I should let you know that we found a floater down in the old Fort. We tried to call ya'll but you know we have no signal down that way."

"Damn!" Was all the sheriff muttered.

ꕥ

Mona packed her bags hurriedly. She left the funeral and headed straight for her house on Dauphine. She didn't stop at the club for fear that one of Marsala's goons would be there. There was a knock at the door. She broke out in a cold sweat. The weather had been sweltering but her knees began to tremble. She looked out of the side window and saw Mr. Renair standing at the door.

She walked quickly to the door. She pulled him in as quickly as she could.

"I was surprised to see your car out front. I thought that you'd be staying someplace else." Mr. Renair seemed surprised by her demeanor.

"I'm leaving. There's trouble and I've got to go." Mona spat out to her old friend.

"I know, that's why I came over." Mr. Renair said calmly.

"What do you mean?" Mona asked.

"I saw some of Tony's men outside here earlier today. Don't panic, they've gone, but they really looked the place over to see if you were here. From my guessing, they'll be back, the dogs." Mr. Renair said angrily.

Mona ran to the window to look out again but there was no one there.

"Go child. Go now." Mr. Renair advised as he headed for the door.

The club was packed with customers. Many locals had come out to support the return to normalcy. All of the band members had returned to their posts. The jazz music which flowed out into the street gave everyone who passed a sense of hope. Sugar Doll climbed up the back stairs to her mother's rooms. The door was locked. She knocked a few times before realizing that no one was there. Perhaps her mother was coming from the Dauphine address. Her gown glimmered in the overhead light. Her caramel skin glowed in the shadows. As she descended the stairs Remy caught sight of her again. She was no longer the girl he had first met. She was truly a woman of great beauty. He felt his heart melt at the sight of her.

"Excuse me Tim, have you seen Mona this evening?"

"No Miss Mona, I haven't seen her today at all." Tim said wiping down the bar glasses. "It ain't like her to miss the grand opening. Maybe ya'll should go to her house to check on her. It's gotten real dangerous around here since the hurricane. Folks is desperate." He sighed and continued wiping down the glass.

"Remy, could you go down to the house for me? I'll start the set and by the time you get back we can do the second set together." Sugar Doll asked.

"Sure honey, anything for you." He winked and walked out the door.

❦

The sheriff stood at the riverbank as they pulled the large tugboat to the shore. He scratched his forehead as he looked out onto the widened mouth of the Mississippi. A lot of land had gotten eaten up in the hurricane.

"Sheriff, the body had a wallet on it. His name was Bertrand Boudreaux." A younger man walked over to the sheriff as he studied the contents of the wallet.

"Bertrand Boudreaux, the owner of Beauchamp's in the French Quarter" the sheriff said. "What in the hell was he doing down here on a damned tugboat I wonder." The sheriff said mostly to himself.

"Maybe he was helping out sir." The younger man offered.

"He was from down here alright but he was a piano man. He never did a bit of work in his life. Something's fishy and it's not just him." The sheriff commented. The younger man laughed.

"I wasn't trying to be funny son. A man is dead. That ups my body count and I don't like it. Search the damned boat." The sheriff barked.

"Right, right." The younger man left his side and gladly joined the other officers and workmen who stood on side of the boat.

Remy approached Mona's darkened house and parked his car. It looked as if no one was there. A car pulled up behind him. He turned to see if it was Mona, but the brights were on and blinded him. A bullet ripped through the back windshield. Remy turned quickly and started the engine as fast as he could. He floored the accelerator and lurched forward but crashed into a street lamp. He jumped out of the car and ran. He could hear footsteps running rapidly toward him. He felt a bullet whiz by his head. He ran into an alley and realized his mistake immediately. It was a dead end.

Chapter Twenty

The club was standing room only. There were politicians there and a few movie stars. This was more than a Grand Re-Opening; this was a statement of defiance from the people. The government had forgotten them but the people had not. The city would return to its fun loving, carefree days, even if it killed them. There was electricity in the air. The surrounding areas were stifled by water damage and devastation but on this night everything was glamour. The jazz band was playing an upbeat tune and whiskey flowed. There was no sign of Mona. Sugar Doll paced nervously in the greenroom waiting to hear from Remy.

"Sugar Doll, you're on honey!" Tommy came back and interrupted her worries. "If only Bertrand was here" she whispered to herself. He was the big teddy bear of a man who eased her troubled mind. His smile and laugh made everything okay. Tonight she would step out without him as her friend, cousin and mentor.

"Ladies and gentlemen, please give a warm applause for the Crescent City's own, Sugar Doll!" She stepped onto the stage as the emcee gave her a hug and a kiss and as she looked out into the crowd something changed in her. She felt strong and brave. "Thank you, thank you and welcome back to New Orleans!"

The crowd burst into a round applause. "In honor of those who lost their lives and to our own wounded hearts I want to sing one you all know." She turned to talk to the band.

"Oh when the Saints go marching in, oh when the Saints go marching in...I want to be in that number, when the Saints go marching in..." As she sang the crowd stood up to second line and pulled out their white handkerchiefs. Tears streamed from faces which were smiling in spite of themselves. The night was magic and the band was on fire.

"Why don't you tell us where the money is and make it easy on yourself and that pretty girlfriend of yours?" Sid stood over Remy holding a gun to the temple of his head.

"What money?" Remy asked bewildered as he glinted up into the bright light that was overhead.

"The money you and your partner Bertrand stole from Marsalas." Sid said gruffly.

"I didn't steal any money. I don't know what you are talking about. I haven't seen Bertrand in weeks." Remy spat out.

"Yeah, at least that boy is smart. He had the sense to run. What you thought you'd just hang around and spend our money?" Sid hit him over the head with the butt of the gun.

Marsalas sat in the darkened corner studying Remy. "The kid don't know nothing. Let him go."

"You sure boss?" Sid asked.

"Yeah, I guess you were right." Marsalas took a sip of his whiskey.

"Get out of here kid." Sid said.

Remy tried to stand but felt weak in his knees.

"Help him." Marsalas ordered.

Sid and one of his goons lifted Remy by his shoulders and carried him to the car. They drove him to the club and threw him out on the curb.

"I guess I don't have to warn you about keeping your mouth shut." Sid growled as he pulled off and sped away. The music inside the club was pumping out to the street. A few people approached him.

"Hey fella, you okay?" One of the people asked as he lifted him up to his feet.

"It looks like they really worked you over. You want me to call the police?" The older man asked.

"No, I'll be alright, it was personal." Remy said as he gathered strength and headed for the door. The club was jammed tight. He decided to go through the side door to cut through the back and cut into the bathroom to get a look at the damage they did to him.

He walked into the men's room. He caught a glimpse of his reflection. "A bit roughed up but none the worse for the wear." He winked at his reflection as he pulled a paper towel out and wet his face to clean at the cut directly above his temple. "A quick move to the right and no more Remy." He mused to himself. He heard the intercession music begin as the crowd became louder and more boisterous. He dried his face and made his way out of the bathroom.

"It's about time!" Sugar Doll stood outside of the bathroom in the hallway waiting for him.

"Hey Sugar." Remy said amiably.

"What the hell happened to you?" Sugar Doll exclaimed once she saw his condition.

"Well, apparently someone thinks I robbed Marsalas." Remy said leaning against the hallway wall.

"What? Why would they think that?" Sugar Doll asked.

"They think that Bertrand and I were in on the robbery here at Mona's." Remy said pointing to the ceiling, as though the building was its own entity.

"Who did this?" Sugar Doll asked.

"Marsalas." Remy answered simply.

"Oh my God. Why did they let you go?" Sugar Doll asked.

"Well dahling, I'm still waiting for you to ask me if I'm all right. I'll try to figure out the rest later." Remy smirked.

"Are you all right?" Sugar Doll stepped forward and took Remy into her arms.

"Five minutes." Tommy the barman interrupted the kiss.

"Five minutes." Remy repeated and straightened out his rumpled shirt.

"I can go on again." Sugar Doll squeezed his arm.

"I'll be all right." Remy smiled as he ambled down the narrow hallway into the crowded bar.

The crowd cheered when he entered the room. Sugar Doll took a deep breath and followed him. They had rehearsed the old standard, "I've Got You Under My Skin" with a New Orleans melody underneath. Remy had taken the stage to begin the first portion of the song. She followed smoothly answering the second chorus. It was magic. The crowd murmured their approval not wanting to interrupt the moment.

"I'm sorry that I'm a little late. I was getting roughed up by some gangsters." Remy joked. The audience laughed appreciatively not realizing that he was telling the truth.

"C'mon Remy you were out with some wild girls and lost track of time." A man in the crowd shouted. The audience laughed raucously.

"There's only one girl for me from now on…" Remy looked admiringly at Sugar Doll. He began to sing a ballad that he had written for her. She sat on a stool as he sang to her.

As locals woke to the morning news of Bertrand's death Marsalas gave a huge sigh. "Stupid nigger. What was he thinking going down into the heart of the hurricane?" He muttered to himself. The police found a briefcase full of money. He couldn't believe his luck. "I knew it was him!" He spat out angrily. He picked up his phone to call Sid. There was a knock at the door.

"I heard boss and I booked it right on over here." Sid stood at his door.

"Well, we ain't getting that money back." Marsalas stood at the window overlooking the business district.

"We can get it from Mona." Sid said.

"Yeah, well, where is she? Your guys lost her." Marsalas asked.

"Whatever is lost can be found boss." Sid replied.

"Like my money?" Marsalas asked sarcastically.

Sid said nothing in response.

Sugar Doll was inconsolable. What she had feared the most was now a reality.

"Oh Remy, why are all of these bad things happening to us?" She asked.

"Sugar, we made it through a hurricane to sing again. Bertrand made some unwise choices and he died. I'm sorry but you can't take all of this on yourself." Remy tried to comfort her.

"First Elise, then Big Ma, Kevin and now Bertrand. It's just too much for me." She cried.

"I'm more worried about Mona now." Remy reminded her. "Marsalas thinks that she was in on the robbery."

"Oh God, I have no idea where she is Remy. How can we help her if we don't know where she is or if she is even still alive?" Sugar Doll cried fresh tears.

"Now listen to me, Mona is smart. She's gone somewhere no one can find her and she is perfectly fine. It's us I am really worried about. If they can't find her then maybe they'll come looking for answers from you. They've already tried me." Remy advised.

"But I don't know anything." Sugar Doll answered.

"They don't know that and I'm afraid that it's time for us to go to the police."

"What are we going to tell the police?" Sugar Doll asked.

"Everything that we know. At least if something happens they will know who the cause of it is." Remy responded.

"But it's dangerous. Marsalas knows everybody and could cause us real trouble." Sugar Doll pleaded.

"It's already dangerous. Doing nothing is not going to help us." Remy told her.

"You know the New Orleans police department is full of crooked cops. Why should they help us?" Sugar Doll sighed.

"Not all of them are crooked. We can get help honey. We can just tell what we know and be fine." He soothed her.

He kissed her neck gently and she responded to him feeling her shoulders relax as he held her closely.

ꕥ

"Give the legal rights to my club to my daughter. She can be chief executor of my assets." Mona spoke to her Southern California attorney. She had come to San Diego a place no one knew that she owned property in because it was under an assumed name. She knew that this was the best place for her because it was oh so close to Mexico, a haven for hideouts.

"When will I tell her?" The attorney questioned this tactic.

"When it's necessary. I can't go back there and I probably won't be around here for long either. You know as well as I do that the Marsalas cartel will try to hang me just for the thought of my being involved even though I'm innocent." She spoke to the attorney urgently.

"Isn't your daughter exposed and in danger?" He asked more worried for the girl than for the feisty Mona he had come to know.

"No, they won't touch her. If you've been watching the news the focus has been on the murders that took place. They would be asking for investigation if they were to try to harm a local celebrity in that way." She felt satisfied with this answer.

ꕥ

Late in the afternoon Sugar Doll sat in the empty club when the phone rang.

"Hello, may I speak to Mona Bouvier?" Came the prim voice of an older woman.

"I'm sorry ma'am but she has been gone for several weeks now. She left me in charge, I am her daughter Precious Bouvier, can I help you with anything?"

"Why yes, it's pertaining to your father and a few unpaid commitments on his part. Your mother was the next person I was to call." The woman spoke as though Sugar Doll's father had just recently died when in fact he'd passed away over twenty years ago.

"I see, and this is?" Sugar Doll asked politely.

"Sister May Ellen McKeckney of St. Francis's School for Girls. I apologize for calling you at such a terrible time as your father's death but you see he donated quite a bit to the school on your behalf and then there was a promised sum of ten thousand dollars which we already had allocated into our budget for the coming year. You mother did tell us of your father's recent death but she said that she would honor the commitment at least for this year." The voice trailed off.

"Recent death," was still resounding in Sugar Doll's head.

"Ma'am are you sure that you are calling the right student? My father Karl Bouvier has been deceased for over twenty years. I was on scholarship at your school during my time there." Sugar Doll responded even though her heart rate had increased.

"Oh, I see." Was all the woman could manage. Sugar Doll heard the phone disconnect and the accompanying dial tone that went with it. She hung up the phone as well and rubbed her temples. Remy had not called in a few hours and since the incident she was worried about him. In her heart all of the questions came rolling back. She looked out of the open window and could smell the orange spray paint that the neighboring store had recently used for their renovations. The scent was as strong now as when they had first done the job in the morning. The aerosol cans were lined up neatly on the side of the building. "That stuff's giving me a headache" she said mostly to herself. The owners were too cheap to buy real paint but the affect was the same on the old building. It did spruce it up a bit.

Sugar Doll decided to take a walk by the river to clear her head. It was still early evening. The street was humming with activity. The nightmare of the hurricane was over and many had returned to the Quarters. After all of the heartache that the city had endured it was difficult to believe that things would ever get back to normal but this day seemed like it had. Everything was normal but the news that she had just received.

"There you go making up lies again." Sugar Doll winced at the memory of other children teasing her for not being black again. They taunted her. The only one who had always defended her was Bertrand. When children made comments about her hair or her hazel eyes he would fight them or push them away. He was the only one who seemed to believe her. The older people in her family blamed it on a recessive gene from the "slave days". Some would cluck behind her back but they were too afraid to say anything in front of Big Ma.

The nun had not given her a name for the father but Sugar Doll knew who she was talking about and had been afraid to say his name. The walk was refreshing and she let her mind wander to Tony. He was a handsome man. As she thought of him she tried to see any resemblance. Had she mistaken his flirting for fatherly love? She'd felt mildly repulsed when he wanted to hug her. She had seen him on his final day. Now she was determined to find out the truth. She thought angrily of Mona now. How dare she leave all of this on her shoulders without once hinting at any answers. She thought of her real father. She recalled that he loved her. He died trying to shield her. Would he do that for a child that wasn't his? She didn't know what to think anymore. She knew what she had to do.

Sugar Doll was just standing on St. Charles Avenue in front of the beautiful house that looked more like a mansion to her. "Big Ma, I know that this is forbidden but I've got to do it. I've got to find out the truth." She spoke softly up toward the sky. She crossed the median where the trolley regularly passed. She knew that once she crossed that line she would not be able to turn back. The fact that the woman she was visiting was probably her sister did not deter her. Her hazel green eyes and golden colored locks suggested something far different than being the daughter of the kind dark skinned man she had always thought of as her father. She held her breath and knocked on the beautiful carvings on the door. She was so nervous that she hit it wrong and her knuckle burned. She saw the door knocker after that and laughed to herself. She needed a little comic relief.

"Hello," a very young girl answered the door and appraised Sugar Doll carefully. She was no more than seven. "You look just like Auntie Celeste the girl smiled. She had never seen Celeste before but had heard of her. She was much older than Sugar Doll perhaps by ten years. She also was Tony's only daughter.

"Who's at that door, Heather?" A voice came from inside the cavernous house.

"A pretty lady." Heather yelled back. She smiled at Sugar Doll then.

"C'mon in…" Heather opened the door wider.

A beautiful woman came around the corner dressed elegantly in a red tight fitting dress that looked to be designer. Her blond hair was pulled up in a French roll and had the retro look of the forties. Her make-up was impeccable and she was lovely. She was a tall woman and had the figure of a model.

"Well, hello, can I help you honey? I'm awfully busy, things are really demanding at the boutique and I just came home to drop off my niece Heather here. How can I help you honey?

Sugar Doll felt suddenly faint and speechless. The woman did look a great deal like her. Her knees grew weak. The older woman sensing that something was wrong grabbed her by the arm and brought her over to the hallway chair.

"Heather go and get her some water. It's awfully hot outside. Honey please tell me that you are not doing door to door in this heat." The woman chuckled amused at her little joke.

Sugar Doll recovered herself.

"I'm sorry; I don't know what to say. Today has been a bit difficult." She managed to say.

Heather returned with the water. "Here you go ma'am"

"Thank you very much." Sugar Doll managed and drank the water quickly. She was ready to go.

"Um, I'm sorry to disturb you but there's been a mistake." Sugar Doll rose to leave.

"Wait a minute honey. There's no mistake. I recognize you now." Celeste said decisively.

"You know me?" Sugar Doll gulped.

"Sure, you are the reason my parents never married. Oh the shame of it." She said playfully and winked.

"So when did you find out?" Celeste smiled benevolently.

"Today, I guess, I figured it out." Sugar Doll answered.

"Nothing like a hurricane to stir up the truth dahling." Celeste stood up straight.

"I've always wanted to meet you but I was forbidden by my mother." Celeste went on grabbing the other chair in the hallway.

"Your mother knew?" Sugar Doll asked surprised.

"Sure she did. They weren't married or anything. She just got, how do you say, "caught"? Well, she's from old money and they wanted nothing to do with that gangster gang over there so they sent her away for awhile and then she came back a war widow...except the soldier wasn't a soldier and he wasn't a husband. People accepted it because I was so pretty. I felt sort of sorry for you though. I figured that you wouldn't have all of the luxuries I had being black and all. You don't look black at all. How did you manage being around them for so long?" Celeste asked sincerely.

"Well, my mother is black. It wasn't a chore and I see now that Tony did take pretty good care of me, considering the times. Did he ever come to see you?" Sugar Doll asked.

"Now and again, when I was a teenager he came quite regularly as a family friend, but I knew. Just like I know that you are my half sister."

"Have you seen photos of me or something?" Sugar Doll asked.

"No, not until recently when you started singing in the French Quarters. You look like him, more than I do." She said appreciatively.

"He had blue eyes." Sugar Doll winced at the comparison.

"Everybody else in his family had green or hazel eyes, like ours. See." She grabbed Sugar Doll by the elbow and took her to a mirror. The resemblance was striking. The only difference was Sugar Doll's tawny complexion.

"Well, thank you so much for your kindness. I won't bother you any longer." Sugar Doll prepared to leave. She was embarrassed and needed to see Remy terribly.

"No bother, I'm just surprised that you didn't know. How did your mother manage that?" Celeste asked.

"My father died when I was young and I lived with my grandmother most of the time." Sugar Doll said.

"Well Darling, we can't help where we come from. I'm a bit older than you but let me give you some sisterly advice. Don't go trying to connect with the Marsalas family, they are bad news and dangerous. You seem to have quite a following from what I've been told. I say stick to your own way and you'll be fine. I'm sorry if I sounded a bit racist back a minute ago. I didn't mean it. Now that we know about each other come by sometime and let's chat. If you ever need anything let me know. My mother left me pretty well off." She smiled kindly at Sugar Doll.

"Thank you, Celeste." Sugar Doll smiled back.

"Heather's right, you are pretty, just like me." Celeste winked.

Sugar Doll left the house feeling disconcerted. Did everyone know? She felt like a fool.

Chapter Twenty-One

The bartender from Iowa received the phone call in his neutral accent. The voice on the other end was immediately recognizable. He hung up after listening to instructions. He gave no response. He looked around but no one was paying him any attention. His job was to watch and report. He wanted to take action but knew that he would only mess things up for everyone involved. There was no sign of Remy. He knew the boy's habits by now and this was not like him.

The FBI was so close to breaking up the Marsalas cartel that it seemed a shame that it was already in danger of imploding. As Tommy wiped down the bar the phone rang again. He grimaced knowing that this phone call wouldn't be about business.

"I know honey; I do want to get married. A lot of things are going on right now. I hate it here, the humidity is horrible. Please be patient. I promise that I'll make you my wife by springtime. He grimaced to himself knowing that the fellas back at the bureau were going to razz him for this. Giving Marla this number had definitely been a mistake. He never knew how much she whined until the teasing had become unbearable. He loved her in spite of this and took the teasing as a rite of passage.

"I gotta go now, the bar's filling up." He hurried his love off of the phone. Sugar Doll walked into the bar and he immediately hung up without saying goodbye. He would live to regret that.

"Hey Tommy, talking to that girlfriend of yours again?" Sugar Doll smiled.

"Fiancé' and yes I'm sorry, she called me this time." He apologized.

"That's quite alright honey. I understand." Sugar Doll stood by the bar but she was looking out the window. Tommy noticed her distraction.

"Can I get you something to drink?" He offered.

"No thanks, hey listen have you seen Remy?" Sugar Doll asked the question but continued to focus on the street.

"No ma'am I haven't seen him all day. He usually stops by at this time." He answered.

"I'm worried Tommy." Sugar Doll bit her lip.

"It's okay; he's probably across the river running errands." Tommy reassured her but made note of the seriousness of the event.

"It's not like him to not call and a few weeks ago some men jumped him." She said this mostly to herself. She turned and headed toward the door to go to the police station.

All of her attention had been focused on ideas to save her mother but now she realized that Remy was the one who seemed to be in the most danger. They had let him go once before so why would they take him again? It didn't make sense. Sugar Doll wondered as she ran out to the street. She walked quickly up St. Ann hoping to catch a taxi. Tommy remained at the bar but he picked up the phone to call that familiar number. "Stop her," was all he said.

"I had this system for getting exactly what I wanted out of people. Over the years that changed. I saw that I couldn't get away with the things I used to so I changed my system." Marsalas sat on a rolling stool in front of Remy. "I don't want to kill you boy but I will. That mother of your whore is out there somewhere and she owes me something. I want you to find out where she is."

Remy shook his head and shrugged his shoulder signifying that he had no idea.

"I know that you don't know but you will find out if you want that pretty girlfriend of yours to live." Marsalas threatened again.

Remy shook his head in understanding. It was late evening when they released him again. He was sore from head to toe. He didn't want Sugar Doll to see him this way. He knew that the police had "ratted him out" to Marsalas. He'd tried to explain the situation to one of the officers down at the station but soon discovered that was a huge mistake. He'd not told of his plans to anyone because he wanted to distance Sugar Doll from any of the trouble.

Remy went to his apartment ready for the barrage of questions but it was empty. He relaxed and took off his shirt. He had a few minor bruises but in all he was okay. He decided that a hot shower would set him right. He went to the fridge to get out a cold beer. It was hot in his usually cool apartment. Sugar Doll had gotten into the habit of turning the air off when she left the building. The heat usually descended in a matter of minutes. The humidity stifled everything. He leaned over the sink and turned the air on full blast.

He felt his wet cuts open in the breeze and headed for a healing shower.

Sugar Doll sat on a bench in the hallway of the police department. She'd come to file a missing person report and the sergeant in charge had motioned for her to wait. She already knew the twenty-four hour rule but was there to break it quite simply by lying. She wondered silently why anyone who had ever watched a movie had not simply lied about the last time they had seen a person. She was preparing to make her story as dramatic as possible. They would have to send out the cavalry because Remy deserved that much. A handsome man approached her and tapped her on the shoulder. She turned to look at him. He was in a nicely cut suit. It was definitely designer by the looks of it. Perhaps even Giorgio Armani. She smiled involuntarily at him.

"May I speak to you for a moment please?" The man politely asked.

"I'm sorry, are you a detective?" Sugar Doll asked but judging from the way he was dressed he was probably a lawyer or something.

"No, I'm not. Would you accompany me outside so that I can tell you who I do work for?" He asked in a slightly lowered voice. The sergeant behind the counter looked up at them but soon lost interest.

"Why can't you tell me right here?" Sugar Doll asked suddenly unusually afraid.

"Okay, if you insist. I'm with the FBI and I know that your boyfriend is at his apartment as we speak. He is safe but you my dear are not." He smiled simply at her shocked expression.

She stood then at his request and walked alongside him as he spoke in quiet and hushed tones.

"Marsalas and his crew are looking for your mother. They have roughed up your boyfriend in the hopes of finding out any new information about her but they are considering taking you next and the outcome may not be so friendly." The man said as he led her down the front stairs of the police station.

"Shouldn't the police know about this?" She asked.

"They do know, that's why your boyfriend has been missing all day. He came to them to try to protect you but in case you didn't already know the police here are corrupt. Were you about to file a missing person's report?" The man asked.

Sugar Doll only nodded.

"Don't do one for Remy, request one for your mother and listen to anything they tell you." The man asked.

"How do I know that you aren't one of Marsala's men?" She asked.

"You don't but here's my badge to help you to believe me." The man took out an FBI id holder.

Sugar Doll studied it and returned it. She walked slowly back up the stairs to wait for assistance. This time with a renewed reassurance that Remy was home and fine.

❦

"My only defense is to write down every word they say." Sugar Doll thought to herself as the police went over the old report about her mother. They had found nothing new, no sightings or anything. Mona had been missing for quite some time. The bar was hers to keep. The officer who went over the report looked at her benevolently. "Don't worry dahling, this is New Orleans and people always come back here. Your mother's just taking a break. It's been quite a year." Just two weeks later there was a mysterious letter which legally gave her ownership of not only the bar but the house on Dauphine. It was a nice house and close enough to the Quarters to walk to work. There was no return address but Sugar Doll felt that it confirmed that her mother was alive and well somewhere.

Mona sat on the beach thinking about all that she had lost. Her mother was gone, her lover was gone and she had lost her connection to the city that she loved. She held a copy of the Times Picayune. There was a lovely photo of her daughter and Remy beautifully decked out on the wedding announcements page. She cried.

"It's official, I've missed all of the most important dates of your life." She stood resolved, dusted herself off and headed toward her hotel.

A light tapping on the window frightened Sugar Doll. The tapping came again. She went to the window to look out into the pouring rain. She rubbed her eyes in disbelief as what seemed like the ghost of her mother wrapped in a coat and scarf peered back in at her. She felt a shock go through her.

She ran to the door not bothering to put on a robe. As she opened the door the rain dripped into the doorway. "Mother!" She gripped her mother in the wet raincoat.

"Sugar Doll," Mona mouthed the words unable to speak. The two women hugged in the doorway. After the initial shock was over they walked to the table.

"Remy?" Mona asked.

"He's in the apartment over the bar. Appearances, you know." Sugar Doll smiled. "Let me make you some coffee." She had already moved into the kitchen to make the brew.

"I'm so happy for you." Mona cried. "I've wanted to come to the wedding but I didn't want to take away from your special day.

"It has been tough actually with Big Ma gone. My favorite members of the family are all missing. Celeste is coming to the wedding surprisingly enough." Sugar Doll looked at her mother to see if this would register any reaction.

"So you know?" she asked simply.

"Yes, I know but I have gotten over the shock. She is very nice indeed. She has already given us a really nice wedding present." Sugar Doll shrugged as she waited for the coffee to brew.

"I'm sorry that I never told you honey. There was shame in it." Mona shrugged out of her coat and put it on a chair next to the table.

"I wish I would have known while he was alive. I would have treated him differently." Sugar Doll pouted.

"We are what we are. You were honest with him. He loved you in his way." Mona looked down at her hands. "We should have been married; perhaps things would have turned out differently." She wiped away a tear.

"Why didn't he want me around?" Sugar Doll asked.

"He knew that it was only a matter of time before Marsalas would see the resemblance. You are the spitting image of Celeste, his oldest daughter. When you were younger you looked more like me. We couldn't be a happy family Sugar. I had to be his whore. That they could accept. Not the mother of his child." Mona sat down heavily.

"Why didn't you leave him?"

"I loved him." Mona stared at her hands.

"What are you doing here? Don't you know that it is still dangerous for you?" Sugar Doll changed the subject. She poured the coffee.

"Yes, that it is but after two long years things must have cleared up. I knew that Tony was using my club as a front for Marsalas but I didn't take massive amounts of money. I just took enough for your future.

"Did Tony know?"

"No, he took his own helping and was only too glad not to get caught. The club was very popular back then so any extra money I had seemed good enough to explain to anyone. No one asked. Tony cooked the books anyway so a few thousand here and there didn't hurt anything."

"So you stole from them?" Sugar Doll asked surprised.

"No more than they stole. That wasn't honest money. I didn't know when Tony would get tired of me and kick me to the curb. I always thought that I'd come back to get you honey and I wasn't coming broke." Mona reached over the counter and touched a lock of Sugar Doll's hair. "After all those years how much do you think you owe Marsalas?"

"It's not just the money baby. I could be a key witness on many things against Marsalas. He doesn't know that I don't want to tell but I will if I have to." Mona shrugged out of her raincoat, water dripping to the floor.

"Well the police have been hauling us in and even the FBI is involved. I didn't understand but it's more than just the club money or the gambling money Bertrand and Kevin tried to take. They just stopped picking up Remy at the end of last year." Sugar Doll sat at the bar to look at her mother. Mona was beautiful and aging very well. "I don't think that you should be here. It's dangerous for all of us." Sugar Doll looked directly at Mona.

"I have no plans for staying. I just needed to take care of a personal matter. I gave the house and the bar to you." "Mona!" Remy stood at the doorway in disbelief.

"Remy." Mona stood calmly.

"You shouldn't be here." Remy leaned against the door.

"Neither should you, it's bad luck to see the bride before the wedding." Mona smiled.

"Well I'm sort of her bridesmaid and lady in waiting." Remy shrugged off his raincoat. "Isn't it dangerous for you to be here?"

Sugar Doll pulled out three cups and began to pour the coffee.

"Yes, no one knows that I am here. As a matter of fact I am here under an assumed name. I wanted to see you honey just one last time. I wanted to see your wedding. I'm so happy for you both." Mona cried.

Remy crossed the room and took Mona into his arms hugging her. She let out a sigh of relief.

"It's been a really tough year for us all."

"Amen to that." Mona gathered her composure and looked at the beautiful couple.

"Quite a ceremony you guys have planned according to the papers." She wiped her tears.

"Yes, many of the musicians in the city are coming down to your bar and we are going to have a regular old jam session.

We don't need a wedding band". Remy grabbed Sugar Doll from behind and kissed her lightly on the neck.

"I wish Tony and I could have been as free with our love but that was a different time back then." Mona sighed again.

"Is it just the wedding that brings you home?" Remy asked.

"Remy, I don't care what it is. I'm just happy to see family." Sugar Doll sat down wiping a tear from her cheek.

"Well Remy, the truth is that I'm homesick. One can only take so much of sandy beaches and rock music. I've come to make a deal with the Feds to help bring Marsalas down." Mona confided.

"Mama no, that's crazy talk. They are going to kill you. Why did you have to come back to do that?"

"I have to testify in open court. They have a few of his men but they really need me. I took all of the books after Tony died. There are notes and dates and even times of transactions. That's what Marsalas has been looking for in the first place. He trusted Tony because they were kin. Ours was a small operation but he had others and Tony took care of a great deal of them."

"Why didn't you come sooner?" Sugar Doll asked.

"Too much going on wasn't there? I would have tried to make a deal with Marsalas himself but he threatened me after Tony died so I just took everything and left. He couldn't find me but the Feds did soon enough and my lawyers negotiated a deal with them."

"Then if they have the deal why have they been harassing us? Even Marsalas has threatened Remy and me." Sugar Doll slammed down her coffee cup.

"They want to make sure that there are no loose ends. The only way that they could get to me is through you. I didn't mean to leave you with all of this trouble but I had no choice. That's why I'm here now. I want to make sure that both of you are safe and sound before I do anything." Mona stood to make her point.

"They'll be looking for you at my wedding. You must realize that. This is the worst time to come." Sugar Doll stood shaking her head.

"You both have to go away for awhile as things are going to get hot and I don't want to take a chance on losing either one of you. After all you are the only family I have now."

"Go away? Where?" Sugar Doll shrieked.

"Europe, somewhere obscure like Holland or Sweden. Places people wouldn't even think of looking." Mona said.

"We can't do that, there's the club." Remy spoke up finally.

"The club will be there when you get back. It's a time to run. I have money here and will get your tickets right away. Use it as your honeymoon present. No one will suspect. I have to go to court on Friday. After that it's going to be dangerous for you both and I can't stand that possibility." Mona cried.

"Why now?" Sugar Doll asked.

"Because the Feds are close to cracking their case against Marsalas and I'm one of their key witnesses. They also have one of his hit men, Sid." Mona said.

"This can't be happening." Sugar Doll said.

"It is happening and you need to deal with it. Now I'm not asking you, I am telling you that you must leave. The police won't bother you anymore. There are Feds watching the house but they can't be everywhere. Your safety is not their primary concern. I came personally because I knew that you wouldn't believe some cop. Please take me seriously." Mona begged.

"At least we would get a real honeymoon Sugar." Remy smiled.

"It's not funny Remy." Sugar Doll said resigned to the idea.

෴

Michael sat down in the middle of the road and began to cry. He had done his best to get out of Marsala's grip. Rudolfo pointed the gun to his head. Just then a warm spring rain began. He felt the rain fall in big droplets on his shoulder. It was surprisingly refreshing considering the fact that he was sweating from the run, the fear and the heat. He couldn't believe that Rudolfo had caught him so easily.

"You are going to die kid." Rudolfo mumbled in his rough voice. Michael saw his mother's face. He cried harder as the rain came down in full force and a gunshot rang out on the empty river road.

෴

"Sam Marsalas?" A policeman walked closely behind the well dressed man.

"You know who I am. Don't play cops and robbers." Marsalas turned to face the officer in front of his business offices.

The officer was joined by two FBI men.

"You are under arrest for conspiracy to commit murder, money laundering and mail fraud." The officer stated as though reading from a script.

Two men stepped out of the office building. "We are Samuel Marsalas's attorneys and we were expecting you." They went to stand beside Marsalas.

"Of course you were" said one of the FBI men. "Cuff him." He instructed the policeman.

"That won't be necessary. Mr. Marsalas is an upstanding citizen of New Orleans and should be treated with the respect he deserves." The older attorney stated standing in front of Marsalas.

"He's a low down killer." Cuff him the FBI said.

In the end Marsalas was led away in handcuffs with his attorneys following closely behind him. Marsalas didn't say anything.

Paster Han and Father Woods presided over the wedding. Remy left the house once Tonya came to pick up Sugar Doll.

"Girl you look beautiful!" Tonya cried as she looked at her gorgeous friend dressed in her lovely satin white gown. It was simple yet elegant and sleek. One strap crossed her shoulder clasped with a diamond heart shaped pin. The gift from Celeste had been her grandmother's. Sugar Doll had her hair pulled back in a beautiful chignon with a simple gardenia clipped to the side in homage to her favorite singer Billie Holiday.

The cathedral was bright and sunny for the mid-day ceremony. The stained glass windows shimmered color throughout the sanctuary. Sugar Doll stood at the doors of the cathedral awaiting the wedding hymn as it had been played during rehearsal. She sighed as she stood alone with no one to walk with her down the aisle. She looked toward heaven. "Big Ma and Betrand I wish you were here with me, but I know that you are in heaven. The doors opened and the church stood to watch the bride. Someone touched her gloved arm. She turned to look and Mona hooked her arm through her daughter's arm. Paster Han came to her right side and held her other arm.

"Now sister you didn't think that we would let you walk down the aisle by yourself." Paster Han smiled. A jazz quartet stood up and began to play "Here comes the bride" with a jazz riff." Her heart soared. Remy stood there smiling as she approached.

"And let the church say Amen!" Paster Han shouted as he walked up to the platform next to Father Wood. Mona took her seat toward the front of the church with tears in her eyes. She saw Celeste who nodded toward her and smiled as she held her young daughter.

"Amen!" The church chorused and laughed as the priest just looked around.

"In the name of the Father and of the Son and of the Holy Ghost" Father Woods intoned. The Catholics made the sign of the cross. The Baptist sat there intrigued but a bit uncomfortable. Remy winked at Sugar Doll. Mona cried. There was a man there dressed in a black suit sitting three seats behind Mona. He was to whisk her away before the reception.

"Do you Remy Gaudeaux take Precious Bouvier to be your lawfully wedded wife?" Father Woods asked.

"Do I get to kiss her then?" Remy smiled. The congregation laughed.

"Yes son, you get to kiss her." Father Woods said seriously.

"Then I do." He leaned in to kiss Sugar Doll.

"Hold on a minute boy!" Paster Han intoned. "I've got to ask her what she wants.

"Do you Precious, Sugar Doll Bouvier take Remy Gaudeaux to be your lawfully wedded husband forsaking all others?" He winked at Remy.

"I….." Sugar Doll was interrupted by Remy's kiss.

"Do."

"Let the church say Amen!" Everyone stood and clapped.

As Sugar Doll exited the church with Remy and flowers seeming to float from the sky she saw Mona being escorted out of the side door. Mona turned to her daughter at that precise moment and mouthed, "I love you." Sugar Doll cried deeply as Remy grabbed her for another kiss.

"The following Friday, Sugar Doll and Remy packed their bags and planned their escape. Mona had gotten the tickets and disappeared just as quickly as she had come to them. Sugar Doll called Tonya to come in to run the bar. She had a business sense and would keep the place going for the weeks they would be gone.

"Stop worrying girl, I'm going to hire a quartet to perform during dinner and maybe a singer in your absence. It will be fine. If anyone asks I'll say that you are on your honeymoon which is as true as it gets." Tonya reassured her friend. The girls embraced.

"Thank you girl, I wish I could tell you everything, but it is better that you are in the dark." Sugar Doll reasoned.

The trial was that morning and it had been decided if they left earlier it would alert Marsalas that something was wrong.

"Are you alright?" Remy asked Sugar Doll as she looked out the tinted window of the black SUV. Tommy was in the driver's seat. His identity had come as a revelation in itself.

"I'm just wondering if we'll ever get back to normal." She cried.

"What is normal honey? Just a setting on the washing machine." Remy cracked smiling at his joke.

"You always make me feel better." Sugar Doll said.

"New Orleans is not the only city in the world you know." He replied.

"Yes, but it's our city." She took his arm and leaned her head on his shoulder. He kissed the top of her head.

They approached the airport. Tommy got their bags out of the truck and went with Remy to check in at the sky cap. They waited in line while Sugar Doll hung back looking nervously over her shoulder. The sky cap took the bag and began to tag it. He looked at Remy in recognition.

"Hey, do you remember that weekend in Duluth?" He asked.

Remy looked behind him to see who the man was talking to and then pointed to himself.

"Me? I've never been to Georgia." Remy replied.

The man stared blankly for a moment. He nodded and then bent down to put the bag on the tram. A shot rang out as Remy stood strangely motionless. He then fell to one knee awkwardly as though he were being invisibly held up by angels. Tommy sprang into action dropping the bags and running toward Sugar Doll. He was hit in the right shoulder as he lurched his body forward to cover the distance between them. He landed on Sugar Doll and they both tumbled to the ground.

"Keep still!" He shouted to her. Remy was still kneeling but he managed to turn toward Sugar Doll. She let out a horrific scream. People began to run into the airport entrance. Sugar Doll watched as Remy's eyes clouded over and became glazed. She saw blood seep from his hairline. She tried to move but Tommy's weight pinned her down. She could taste her lipstick first and then blood.

"Let me go!" She screamed crying. Tommy wouldn't budge.

"It's my job to protect you." He gritted through his teeth. In moments squad cars flooded the upper floor departure portion of the airport. Shots rang out in the nearby garage but they were distant.

"Put your hands over your head!" An officer commanded Tommy who was struggling to hold Sugar Doll down.

"FBI!" He shouted reluctantly releasing Sugar Doll and reaching for his badge evident on his belt. Sugar Doll crawled toward Remy. He was unconscious.

Mona's testimony had damaged Marsalas but she learned during the trial that a simple gunman named Michael had signed sworn affidavits of his involvement in at least three murders and the extortion of at least six public officials. He was not at the trial but his mother had come and testified to her son's signatures. She had even implicated Marsalas in her son's disappearance.

"He came to me in a dream. He told me to look for him down by the old river road." Michael's mother testified. On a lark the District Attorney's office sent a few officers out there to investigate and they found his body next to a tree. He was holding a crucifix. Marsalas was indicted on twelve counts of money laundering, three murders and four counts of extortion. He sat wooden as the charges were brought against him.

Mona left immediately after the trial. The Marsalas family was still powerful and she feared for her life. Sugar Doll was unafraid.

"Hey dahling...you still want to go to Holland or France?" Remy smiled from his hospital bed. Sugar Doll leaned in to kiss him as he wrinkled his nose.

"You look like a civil war victim" She laughed.

"Yeah, getting shot in the head will do that to a person." Remy cracked.

"It's a good thing that you have a hard head." Sugar Doll smiled seriously kissing his cheek.

"What's the doctor say?" Remy asked.

"You were lucky. One more inch and no more Remy. The angle of the shot was what saved you. You will sing again though." Sugar Doll smiled.

"I want to do more than sing sugar." He wiggled his eyebrows suggestively.

"Do you think it's over now?" She asked her eyes reflecting concern.

"Dahling, we're public figures. They don't want to mess with us. Besides we had nothing to do with Tony's mess, Bertrand's trouble or Mona's testimony. We should just focus on our singing career." Remy reassured her.

"And our growing family." Sugar Doll smiled down at Remy.

Remy tried to sit up but grimaced in pain and lowered himself back to his pillow. "A baby?" He smiled.

"I hope that he can sing." Sugar Doll smiled as well.

"Oh he's going to be a drummer baby." Remy reached for Sugar Doll's hand.

Kalua Lauber is a writer and teacher who currently lives in California with her husband Celso and young son Celsinho. This is her first novel. She has a Master's Degree in English and Secondary Education. She grew up in rural Louisiana and the tragic events of Hurricane Katrina inspired this story. She hopes one day to return to her home state.

CPSIA information can be obtained
at www.ICGtesting.com
Printed in the USA
LVHW021547061120
670969LV00010B/881